OKEY NDIBE

ARROWS OF RAIN

Heinemann

Heinemann is an imprint of Pearson Education Limited a
company incorporated in England and Wales, having its registered
office at Edinburgh Gate, Harlow, Essex, CM20 2JE.
Registered company number: 872828

www.heinemann.co.uk

Heinemann is a registered trademark of Pearson Education Limited

First published by Heinemann Educational Publishers in 2000

British Library Cataloguing in Publication Data
A catalogue record for this book is available from the British Library.

Library of Congress Cataloging-in-Publication Data
Ndibe, Okey.
    Arrows of rain / Okey Ndibe.
      p.   cm. — (African writers series)
    ISBN 0-435-90657-7
    I. Title. II. Series.
  PR9320.9.K56K53 2000
  823 — dc21   98-9591
                        CIP

AFRICAN WRITERS SERIES and CARIBBEAN WRITERS SERIES and
their accompanying logos are trademarks in the United States of America
of Heinemann: A Division of Reed Publishing (USA) Inc.

Cover design by Touchpaper
Cover illustration by Fletcher Sibthorp
Author photograph by Holly M. Williams

Phototypeset by SetSystems Ltd, Saffron Walden, Essex
Printed by Multivista Global Ltd

ISBN 978 0 435 90657 3

08   10 9 8 7 6 5 4

*To E., my mother, and in loving memory of C., my father,
noble parents with whom God flattered an undeserving son; to
A.B. and Doris Fafunwa, magnificent parents-in-law; and to
Sheri, wife and friend, for uncommon love and sacrifice.*

The author would like to thank Wole Soyinka, John Edgar Wideman and Michael Ekwueme Thelwell, for generous encouragement and faith; Abdulaziz Ude, a benefactor; Chinua Acheb for opening my eyes to the beauty of our stories; and Jim I for championing this harvest.

PART ONE

Mists

Chapter One

The young woman lay on the sands, her mouth frozen in a smile, as if nothing in the whole world surpassed the sweetness of death. Her face was hardy, but death made her seem older and sadder than twenty. Her eyes bulged glassy, like a grasshopper's. Her bright blue shirt and skimpy flamingo skirt hung loosely about her, rent. A large copper earring dangled from her left ear. Patterned into the circle was the image of an eagle in the attitude of flight. Her right ear was bare, bloody.

Eyes stared at the sprawled body. For a moment I was tempted to manoeuvre my way to the front, to ask questions and take notes. But a force from within me restrained this urge. The scene was too stark, the crowd's voyeurism too unnerving. Sweat ran in streaks under my shirt, cold and tingly. I put my notebook under my arm and clasped it tight. This was my first sight of a dead body, and I seemed paralysed. In quick succession, my emotion changed from shame to anger to fear. The dry cold wind of harmattan blew lazily into my ear, soft like the hum of a lover's breath. I began to move my toes in small circles against the grains of sand in my shoes. The sand's coarse tactility gradually restored my calm.

Near the corpse stood a lifeguard named Lanky, a man with an athlete's body, taut muscles, and veins that criss-crossed the length of his arms. The crowd formed a semi-circle around him, listening enrapt to his story, told with the fervour of an unlikely raconteur surprised with a captive audience. His hands chopped the air and pointed, conjuring up emotions and events that seemed beyond the reach of his words.

Whenever more people joined the crowd, Lanky retold the story for their benefit. He rendered each telling slightly differently, modulating his voice, mixing in pidgin, altering details, padding events, adding new insights, conjectures, rhetorical questions, sprinkling in proverbs for flavouring, his hands all the while deft in the air, kneading their own tales.

He had just concluded when a group of Europeans who knew him strolled onto the scene. One of them, a pudgy man with a wrestler's body and freckles on his shoulders and face, spoke first.

'Gosh! It's rather early to have a drowning customer, isn't it, Lanky?'

The rest of his party, two men and a blonde woman, laughed with the freedom of people who had spent much of the night drinking. The crowd fixed the revellers with shocked glares, but the Europeans were not in the least perturbed. Instead, the blonde, high-shouldered, ample-breasted but lean in a near-famished, weight-loss fanatic sort of way, became so titillated she began to cough.

'Obviously not, Dan! Obviously not,' she said between spasms. 'It's never too early for a lifeguard to have a customer. I mean, Lanky here has to earn his living!'

'Hear! Hear!' exclaimed one of the men. Another, his head bald and bony and his chest covered with white hair, spoke in a contrived tone of sympathy.

'Bloody awful to die on New Year's Day. How did this calamity come about?'

The lifeguard's lips quivered with a quick smile and his eyes became radiant as he mounted the orator's platform once again.

'My mouth cannot tell everything my eyes saw today. To God!' he swore, dipping his index finger lightly on his tongue

4

and lifting it skyward. 'I got here at seven sharp.' He raised his left wrist half-way to his face and with his right hand tapped where he might have worn a watch had he owned one. 'Seven sharp. Next year will make it six years since I started this job. Six good years,' he stressed, raising the requisite number of fingers. 'A few months ago the corpses of prostitutes began to appear on beaches like poisoned fish. I never thought that one day I would see one with my two eyes. But this morning I saw *this* one.' He paused, pointing to the corpse.

'True true, it was a big shock. Imagine it: a black woman drowning at seven sharp! If it had been an *oyibo* woman, no surprise at all. Many many *oyibo* who work at the embassies like to swim early in the morning. Like you people,' he said, indicating the four Europeans. 'Some American businessmen and tourists who stay at Hotel Meridian also come out for early morning swims. I used to wonder why *oyibo* people don't fear cold water. But an American tourist told me about a weather in their country that's as cold as the inside of a fridge. I think they call it . . .'

'Winter!' shouted the blonde.

'Aha, winter!' Lanky echoed. 'I even heard it can be colder than a fridge. Imagine that! That's how I knew that what we call cold here is like a joke to *oyibo* people. As for us, cold can make us panic. Before we come out to swim, we make sure the sun has woken up well well and cleared the clouds from its eye. When the sun has warmed the water fine fine, that's when we come out to swim.'

He paused again, as though searching for an appropriate tone.

'I came to work at seven sharp and heard a terrible sound. It was the sound of a drowning person. My spirit-voice told me there was no hope. The harmattan was heavy: I could not even see my hand in front of my face. The sound came again, sharper and louder. Then my spirit somersaulted and told me to do my job, whether there was hope or not. I wiped my eyes and looked in front, no blinking. Still, I saw nothing. That's when my spirit told me to trust my ears. I was about to dive into the water when I saw a ghost rising out of the waves. I nearly peed on myself. To God! But the ghost took a man's shape and even spoke words I was too afraid to hear. Then I saw it was Bukuru the madman. I began to shiver. Everybody knows he's the boyfriend of Mammy Water, the water spirit. True true, I wanted to run away. But the drowning woman cried out again and my spirit-voice reminded me of my duty. I stepped into the water.

'I swam madly to shake away fear. The waves played tricks on me, moving the woman from place to place. I went *fim* this way and her cry came from another direction, so I swam *fam* that way. *Fim, fam, fim, fam*, like fish. By the time I found her she had swallowed so much salt water she was as heavy as a cow. Imagine the likeness!

'You see that spot where a wave is rising?' Lanky thrust out his hand towards the ocean, as though expecting his concentration to freeze the spot. 'Yes, right *there*! That's where I found her. Her belly was like this,' he said, clasping his hands in front of his belly. 'Like a woman pregnant with twins. Yet I managed to bring her out. As I pressed her belly softly softly, horrible sounds came from her mouth and nose. Death had already entered her body and taken a seat.'

Lanky paused again, to let his audience absorb the details. Some of them seemed to despair of his long-winded style, but were in no hurry to move on; nothing on the beach that New Year morning rivalled the spectacle of a smiling corpse. Others seemed entranced by Lanky's strange commingling of ocean tales with the story of the drowned woman.

Lanky looked up at the sea of clouds, then spoke in a mournful tone. 'God who lives in the sky. God knows I did my best. But it was not easy to fight death alone. If there had been anybody to help me, we would be telling a happier story now.' He shook his head, slowly, sadly, seeming to fight back tears.

'When I looked around, do you know who I saw? Bukuru the madman! He stood close to us, sharply watching the woman. The woman turned towards Bukuru. They looked at each other like ghosts sharing silent secrets. The woman opened her mouth – to laugh, I swear! Something choked her, so she only smiled. Then she began to shiver: *jijijiji*. The madman turned and walked away, saying something I did not understand. The woman became quiet. Still smiling, but dead.'

The spectators remained silent, their gaze on the corpse. In the quiet, the roar of the ocean became buoyant, a belch from an old, far-away world. A young girl's cry pierced the silence. She and her mother had just arrived at the scene.

'Mummy! Mummy!' she shouted, her eyes wide with bewitchment.

'Ssssh! Sssh!' the embarrassed woman hushed in vain.

'Will this dead woman . . .'

'Ssh!'

'. . . go to hell?'

'Ssh!'

'Didn't you say . . .'

'Ssh!'

'that bad people . . .'

'Ssh!'

'. . . go to hell?'

'Shut up!'

The girl trembled, then burst into tears.

'Wait till we get home, silly weaverbird!' thundered her mother, pulling her away.

The new silence was brief. Lanky said, 'Why would a dying

woman smile? Perhaps she saw the home of the dead and liked it more than this wretched life.'

There was a confused chatter, then an old man with a dome of grey hair gained ascendancy over the contending voices.

'She's an *ogbanje*. Only an *ogbanje* would smile at death. I'm certain of that.'

'What's an *og ... og ... o-g*?' asked a man in a husky American accent, stumbling on the word. 'What does it mean, the word you used?'

'*Ogbanje*. They can die and return to life over and over again. To them, death is a game, that's why they can laugh at it. Death only means a brief visit to the land of spirits. Then they return to this life.'

'How does a dead person return to life?' asked the American.

'It's a secret known only to *ogbanje*,' asserted the old man. 'And most prostitutes are *ogbanje*. That's why they live the way they do. Their bodies are like borrowed things, so they use them anyhow, without regret. To come and to go is the way of *ogbanje*. It's the music they dance to.'

'Good for them,' said one of the Europeans. 'Wouldn't mind being one of these *ogbanje* characters, myself.'

'Not much hope of that,' the blonde woman said. 'I'm afraid when the curtain comes down on *you* it'll be for good – in more than one sense.' She laughed tipsily at her own witticism, and others in her party joined in.

Perhaps it was the facetiousness in their attitude that provoked the outburst from someone just behind me in the crowd.

'The dead don't envy the living!' rang the powerful voice.

Everybody turned to look. It was Bukuru the madman! He stood, unmoved by the eyes that rained on him. His hair was knotted into long gritty locks that dropped like a rastafarian's to the small of his back. His eyes were deep-set, the colour of an old lake. Wisps of hair sprouted from his nose above his matted moustache. His toes, long estranged from shoes, strained apart from one another. A strand of cloth held up his trousers. His grimy shirt fluttered lightly in the wind. His stink was musty and doughy, like the sea's smell.

He was one of the monsters in my childhood dreams, dreams in which a figure much like him chased me across wide veldts and over jagged hills to the edge of precipices; dreams in which I felt myself tripping, slipping, falling – only to awake to the shame of having peed again in bed, the piss still warm, quickly turning cold.

'He knows something about the woman's death,' Lanky said, pointing at Bukuru. 'Otherwise, what was he doing around where she drowned?'

A din of voices tried to answer, but they were drowned out by the shrill commotion of an ambulance as it hurtled into view, flashing its bloody lights.

Bukuru took in the scene with the passivity of a statue, as if his mind were focused on more lasting things: the rays of the sun, the wind's song, the waves which continued to rise and fall, making eternal love to the shore.

Chapter Two

Another vehicle soon arrived at the scene – a police car, siren wailing. Three homicide detectives jumped out and crossed briskly to the spot where the corpse lay. Their dark glasses gave their faces an impersonal appearance.

One of the detectives began to interview Lanky, scribbling notes as the lifeguard gave long answers to short questions. Without interrupting his writing the officer shouted orders at the other two detectives. They ran hither and thither, now clicking their cameras, now throwing tapes down to take measurements. The crowd observed these rituals from a safe distance.

In repeating his story to the detective Lanky smuggled in details he had not mentioned in earlier tellings, constantly pointing to Bukuru. The madman maintained a posture of detached indifference, his eyes fixed on nothingness.

I knew the detectives' exertions had about an equal chance of leading them to the root of the mystery or ending in vain, another unsolved death, assigned a bureaucratic number and filed away somewhere, to gather dust, soon forgotten. At last, done with their measurements and with questioning Lanky, the detectives approached Bukuru.

'Good morning,' the most senior detective said to him.

Bukuru neither spoke nor blinked.

'I said, good morning,' the detective repeated.

Bukuru cast a glance at the three of them; a wordless acknowledgement, but nothing more.

'What's your name?' the detective asked.

'I have no name,' said Bukuru.

'What do you call yourself?' persisted another officer.

'Nothing. I don't have that need.'

'What do your friends call you?' asked another detective.

'Oh, friends.' He raised his head as if in thought. 'Different things. Depends.'

'Say one. One name,' the detective goaded.

'That's between my friends and me,' said Bukuru.

'Names shouldn't be a secret,' said the chief detective.

'Mine are not secret to my friends.'

'We're officers of the state,' the chief detective announced in a grave tone. 'That's why we ask. In the name of the state.'

'Good. The state is not one of my friends.'

'You should regard us as friends. My name is John Lati.' The chief detective extended his hand; when Bukuru ignored it he nodded to one of his colleagues.

'Douglas Okoro,' said the second detective.

'Abdul Musa,' said the third.

Bukuru refused their outstretched hands.

'Let's leave names aside, then,' said John Lati. 'What do you know about the drowned woman?'

'I tried to save her.'

'Yes?'

'But I failed.'

'Was she in some kind of trouble?' asked Lati.

'She had been raped.'

Okoro asked, 'Did you see who raped her?'

'Yes, I saw them. From a distance.'

'You mean there were more than one?'

'Yes.'

The detectives looked tensely about them. Seeming for the

12

first time to notice the presence of eavesdroppers, they drew Bukuru out of earshot.

◆

The dead woman was carried into the ambulance. The siren's wail came on again as the vehicle drove away. When the sound subsided Lati wagged his finger at Bukuru, who stood arms folded, mouth clasped shut. Okoro produced a pair of handcuffs. Bukuru offered up his hands.

As Bukuru was led to the detectives' car many spectators drew their cameras and clicked away while others spattered him with questions.

'Are you cooperating with the police?'

'Is it true you're Mammy Water's lover?'

'Did you cheat on Mammy Water?'

'Did Mammy Water kill the woman?'

'Are you a madman?'

'Is Bukuru your true name?'

He walked on, answering no one, and was soon sandwiched between Lati and Okoro in the back of the police car. The siren came alive, then the car sped away, driven by Musa, in the direction of the police headquarters in Moloney in the heart of Langa.

The siren's wail became faint, then faded away into the distance. In its wake the familiar sounds of the beach returned. The waves rumbled. Men and women giggled and talked excitedly and played tag games. Children enacted water fights, threw sand at mock fiends and foes, and waded into the waves. Observing the gaiety, I could not detect any sense that, moments before, a corpse had lain on the sands.

Seized by a desire to leave the scene, I made for the bus terminal – a noisy, smelly, bustling place – and boarded a bus for Moloney. The bus was a patchwork of scrap metal, the rusty welding burst apart at too many seams, exposing sharp edges. Inside, the bus was choked with passengers. Like most of them I stood, my right hand clasping a bar above my head. The bar was smooth and slippery with sweat, but it served to keep me stable when the bus lurched.

During the journey the bus grew hot. Then a rowdy contest for the passengers' attention developed between a travelling medicine salesman and an itinerant preacher. The salesman's wares included an antibiotic dubbed 'No more sufferhead' made by 'India's medical wizards', able to cure 'bad spirit and witch-craft, eczema, crawcraw, gonorrhoea, syphilis, AIDS, watery sperm and dead penis'. It sold briskly. The preacher tried to keep pace, undeterred by a passenger's joke about his 'rainy mouth'.

After a while, my mind detached itself from my surroundings, then focused on the bizarre challenge of this, my first assignment as a reporter. My editor's words resonated in my thoughts.

◆

'New Year's Day is bad for news,' the news editor had said in his soft, slow manner. 'Even criminals tend to take the day off. But the business of informing our readers must go on. If we have to squeeze news out of stone, so be it.'

Pausing, he had furrowed his brows. His face wore the look of a man weighed down by all the sorrowful news he had spent thirty-three of his fifty-four years bringing to readers.

'Here's what I want you to do,' he continued. 'Get out to B. Beach early tomorrow. Interview a sizeable number of people. Get a sense of their reactions to this latest farce. Find out how they plan to cope with life under our perpetual leader. Give me your findings by 7 p.m. – in a sharply written feature of no more than one thousand five hundred words.'

I understood that the farce in question was the announcement, to be made on New Year's Day, that, with immediate effect, General Isa Palat Bello would assume the title of Life-President of the Federal Republic of Madia. The farce had little to do with the new title, which was superfluous enough, there being nobody in the country who seriously expected His Excellency, after a brutal reign of twenty years, to hand over power to any force less ultimate and compelling than death itself. The ghastly joke lay in the regime's claim that 99.5 per cent of Madians had voted affirmatively in a referendum, thus compelling Bello to confer the title upon himself.

◆

At police headquarters the female press officer smiled broadly when I introduced myself.

'We have a fantastic scoop for you,' she said. 'Our men just solved one of our most important cases.' Then she pulled a press release from a file and handed me a one-page statement marked STOP PRESS!!

> Crack homicide detectives from the Madia police
> headquarters this morning arrested a suspect in the death
> by drowning of an unidentified woman at B. Beach. The
> suspect, who refused to give his name and whose age has
> not been determined, is of no fixed address. He confessed
> to investigators that he was the last person to see the
> deceased alive.
>
> The suspect may also be responsible for the recent spate
> of rapes and murders at several city beaches. All the

victims are believed to be prostitutes. Investigators believe that the suspect lured his victims to a beach, then raped and killed them.

The investigation will continue in order to gather more evidence. The police encourage anybody who may have any relevant information to contact the nearest police station.

'I can't believe this,' I said, oblivious of the officer's presence.

'What?' she asked.

'I have one or two questions about this release.'

At once her manner changed. 'I'm not authorised to answer any press questions.'

'But . . .'

'Sorry. I can't talk to you.' She disappeared into an inner office. The door clanged shut after her.

◆

After writing the first sentence, I sat staring at the keyboard, my fingers cold with inertia. The story seemed too large and unwieldy to be pinned down. Search as I might, I could find no words with which to achieve a reporter's distance. My mind swirled with images: the dead woman's improbable smile, Lanky's myth-making, the detectives' vigour, Bukuru's calm. A phrase from the news release reverberated in my head: *All the victims are believed to be prostitutes.* Prostitutes. The noun was strangely potent and familiar. It reminded me of the word orphan. The word illegitimate. It reminded me of my own past.

'How's the story coming out?' The news editor's voice gave me a jolt.

'I have it all in my head.'

'Type it out. You're paid to be a reporter, not a memory chip.'

I threw my head down and began to write.

◆

Waking up after a sleepless night, I jogged to a newsstand for the morning papers. Bukuru's arrest was the second most prominent story in all of them. In keeping with the law, the front pages were devoted to His Excellency's new year broadcast.

> His Excellency proclaims self president for life. Releases
> 120 political prisoners as a gesture of his statesmanship
> and generosity. Wishes Madians to know that he is still the
> sun, rising and setting with unfailing regularity. That he
> steadily sees all the traitors; all the patriots, too. All
> saboteurs and colluders with imperialist agents working to
> undermine the Madian nation will be fished out and
> thoroughly dealt with. All patriots will be rewarded. His
> Excellency predicts that 1988 will be a year of plenty for
> all. His Excellency guarantees a bountiful harvest this year.

Ten years ago, to mark the tenth anniversary of his rule, a decree was promulgated which made it an offence for any editor to use a story whose length or prominence upstaged a presidential pronouncement or deed. The offence was punishable according to the discretion of a special tribunal by a minimum of five years in jail.

No editor trifled with the decree. Not since three years ago when one of their number paid a stiff price for breaching the law. A public housing unit in Port Harcourt had caved in during

17

the night, killing twenty-nine people in their sleep, among them a family of five. Moved by the enormity of the tragedy, the editor of a regional newspaper had used the story in the forbidden fashion: he had made its headlines bolder than a report of His Excellency's opening speech to a conference of farmers. The reckless editor was duly arraigned before the News Use Miscellaneous Tribunal. The tribunal's military chairman, a small-headed giant named Brigadier Tipa Panizi, spent an hour shouting imprecations at the hapless editor before imposing a sentence of six years' hard labour.

My story appeared on the *Chronicle*'s second page. I read it with the haste of a bureaucrat skimming an official document. Then I turned to the other newspapers.

The government-owned *Sentinel* published a report headlined 'Serial Murder Case Solved!' There were two photographs: one of Lanky, bare-bodied and smiling, the other of Lieutenant John Lati, spare and sad-faced. Bukuru's impending arraignment, wrote the paper, would create a precedent, being the first time 'somebody who may be a madman will stand trial for culpable rape and homicide'. Then it boasted that 'the law in Madia is truly no respecter of persons – not even the crazy'.

Chapter Three

Two weeks later Bukuru's trial began before a Langa high court. The day was hot and humid.

I arrived at the court at 7 a.m. Cars and buses already filled the parking lot. Many buses bore the colourful logos of newspapers and magazine publishers as well as radio and television stations. Photographers dashed here and there, cameras hoisted on their shoulders, flashing explosions of light at the crush of spectators. Several television cameras were mounted outside the courthouse. Their operators turned them now this way, now that, like anti-aircraft weaponry. The crowd steadily grew in size and rowdiness.

At a few minutes past 8 a.m. the court door was opened. The crowd rushed forward in a wave that overwhelmed the police cordon. One police officer lay on the ground, cradling his ribs, groaning. Incensed, the others began to swing their cowhide whips. Those stung by the whips ran in every direction, letting out squeals of pain.

A police officer speaking through a portable microphone asked reporters to come forward, their picture identity in hand, and file into the courtroom. I detached myself from the crowd and moved towards the police line. Two policemen checked my press identity, then waved me in. Inside the courtroom the reporters were herded to a corner, standing room only.

After we were settled in, the gate was opened to a throng of spectators who rammed their way in until the stifling courtroom was packed full. The previous day the *Madia Gazette* had predicted a large turn-out. In a lengthy preview the paper had disclosed that a crew of reporters had arrived from London to cover the trial for the British Broadcasting Corporation. The West Africa correspondent of the *New York Times* was also expected to report on the trial. The *Gazette* disclosed that many Madian civil servants, determined to attend the trial in person, had bribed doctors' clerks in order to obtain false sick slips.

At 9:15 four detectives led Bukuru into the courtroom. His entry caused a quiet commotion as many spectators raised themselves on their toes, straining to catch a glimpse of him.

The trial was scheduled to begin at 9:30 but at 9:45 neither the prosecutors nor the judge had entered the courtroom. A wall clock behind the judge's bench ticked monotonously; two ceiling fans stirred the stagnant air with creaky revolutions.

At 9:50 the main courtroom door squeaked open and the two prosecuting counsel walked in, severe in their dark, cape-like robes. With his long hair and unkempt beard, Bukuru seemed out of place among the lawyers in their old-fashioned wigs. Very soon the lawyers began to fan themselves with papers.

At 10:06 an air of apprehension spread through the crowd. The clerk bellowed, 'Court!' and a hush fell. In the silence heavy, measured footsteps could be heard approaching the courtroom.

A uniformed orderly opened the door that led to the judge's chamber and stood aside, frozen at attention. Justice Primus Kayode squeezed through the door, a tall, bulky man, bespectacled. This was the one the lawyers called the Elephant. The name alluded to the judge's size; but it also had to do with his tendency to bear down on whoever was within sight whenever his mood was in 'bad weather'. Lawyers and accused alike dreaded the Elephant's hectoring style and it was rumoured that if he found a defendant's face or manner disagreeable, regardless

20

of evidence indicating innocence or guilt, he was wont to convict and impose a harsh sentence.

Justice Kayode cleared his throat noisily and deposited the phlegm in a paper towel. His motions seemed those of a man aware that the eyes of the world were on him. He looked up and surveyed the crowded courtroom. If he was impressed or perplexed, his expression did not show it: his triple-chinned face had that practised look of blankness cultivated by men whose business it is to read others' faces while taking care to mask their own state of mind.

'Clerk!' he shouted.

'Your Honour, Sir!' answered the clerk, the response at once rehearsed and startled, as if there could be no getting used to the Elephant's booming summons. The clerk was middle-aged, bald and portly, like a scaled-down version of the judge.

'Have you established protocol with all the parties in this case?'

'Yes, Your Honour.'

'Call the case.'

'Case number CH847-LSP 33902. The State vs. Mr X., male, adult, of no ascertainable address. Count one: That you, the accused, on 1 January 1988 at approximately 7 a.m., contributed, by acts of omission or commission, to the death by drowning at B. Beach of a human female, age unknown, of no ascertainable address, thereby committing a crime punishable pursuant to the provisions of the penal code number six, sections 4 and 5 (as amended) by death or up to a lifetime in jail.

'Count two: That you, the accused, on 1 January 1988 at approximately 7 a.m., unlawfully assaulted the said deceased in a physical and sexual manner prior to her death, thereby committing a crime punishable pursuant to the provisions of the penal code number five, sections 8 and 9 by up to fifteen years in jail.

'Count three: That you, the accused, on 1 January 1988 at approximately 7:15 a.m., aided and abetted the death of the aforementioned deceased by hindering her resuscitation, thereby committing a crime punishable pursuant to the provisions of the penal code number six, sections 8, 9 and 10 by up to five years in jail.'

'Is the accused ready to enter a plea?' asked the judge, looking morosely in Bukuru's direction.

'Yes, Your Honour.'

'Do you understand the charges?'

'Yes, Your Honour.'

'Have you sought the advice of counsel? I have it in my notes that you have chosen to defend yourself. But the charges are serious, I must have you know. In the circumstances you would be well advised to engage a lawyer.'

'I can't afford one.'

'I understand that a number of lawyers had offered to provide you with free counsel.'

'My case is beyond a lawyer's understanding.'

Justice Kayode's face grew sour. He fixed Bukuru with reproving eyes.

'I have no wish to waste time. I have advised you to accept legal help. It is for you to decide whether to follow my advice. Meanwhile to business. The charges have been read. How do you plead? Guilty or not guilty?'

'Not guilty.'

Lanky the lifeguard was the prosecution's first witness. His answers were so long-winded that on two occasions Justice Kayode warned him to respond more succinctly. The third time the judge raised his voice. 'For the last time, cut out the cock and bull and get to the point!' Lanky lost his composure. He stuttered and stammered and became so fidgety and incoherent that the prosecutor cut short his examination.

'You may now cross-examine the witness,' Justice Kayode said to the accused.

'I do not wish to. The witness said nothing of importance,' said Bukuru.

'May I warn you, Mr X,' thundered the Elephant, 'that such decisions are to be made by me. You understand? By me, exclusively!'

A forensic pathologist was next to take the stand. He testified that medical evidence indicated that the deceased woman had been raped. 'She had sustained substantial lacerations to her labia minora, labia majora, clitoris and vestibule. The injuries were multiple and devastating, consistent with persistent forced entry and penetration with a penis or some sharper object.'

The pathologist testified that the alkalinity of the seawater had compromised the integrity of the semen sample taken from the victim. He also told the court that he could not determine whether the wounds had been inflicted by one attacker or several.

Bukuru waived his right to cross-examine the witness.

The prosecution then called a psychiatrist. He wore a pair of thick reading glasses and entered the witness box with a stack of files in the crook of his arm. The prosecutor, Jerome Okadi, asked him to summarise his findings.

'After several sessions with the accused,' began Dr Mara, 'I found him to be quite discerning, lucid and possessed of rational faculty.'

'Is there any way of determining that somebody is deranged even before you've had the opportunity to make a clinical evaluation of their mental state?'

'No. You might suspect it, but the determination of neurosis, psychosis and other schizophrenic conditions is usually dependent on clinical examination. That's the only professionally sound and respectable procedure.'

'You mentioned suspicion. When would you suspect some-body of derangement?'

'When a person appears – and appears is the key word – to operate outside the established and reasonable norms of his society. It could be in his manner of dressing, speaking, eating, or in some other aspect of demeanour.'

'When you first met the accused, did you suspect him of derangement?'

'No, not really.'

'Would you say, then, that his appearance was within accept-able social norms?'

'No, it wasn't. But I was asked to do a professional evalua-tion, so I had to approach the task with extreme objectivity.'

'But if you had met him in the street?'

'I certainly would have considered him somewhat peculiar.'

'Why?'

'Because of his appearance. The unkempt and untidy nature of his appearance.'

After a pause, the prosecutor put another question.

'You have positively determined that the accused is not men-tally incapacitated?'

'Yes.'

'Beyond the shadow of a doubt?'

'Yes.'

'Briefly, in layman's language as far as possible, kindly outline to the court the basis of your conclusions.'

'The suspect's logical coherence. His ability to recall events in an ordered way. His exhibition of mature speculative reasoning. His ability to comprehend information and to communicate in a clear and meaningful sense. Finally, his ability to make connec-tions – in other words, his cognitive grasp of cause and effect.'

'Is there perhaps a chance that the accused suffered a momentary lapse of mental capacity at the time that he committed the alleged crime?'

'I considered that possibility. However, my finding is not consistent with that theory.'

'Why not?'

'Because of the suspect's near-perfect recollection of the incident. And because of his willingness to discuss the details of the drowning and everything that happened up to his own arrest. When he did not discuss certain details he made it clear he did not wish to talk about them; it had nothing to do with gaps in his recollection. That level of awareness rules out the possibility of a temporary lapse of mental competence – an occurrence that is usually marked by cognitive dissonance and other disassociative symptoms.'

'If the accused was never mentally incapacitated, how would you account for his, as you said, unkempt and untidy appearance?'

'I would describe him as socially maladjusted.'

'And the cause of this maladjustment would be?'

'Maladjustment may spring from a number of factors. There is no need to speculate in this particular case. The most important thing is to underline that social maladjustment is often a matter of choice on the part of an individual.'

'Thank you. No more questions.'

'Mr X,' said the judge, 'I take it you have no questions for the witness?'

'Yes, I do, Your Honour,' Bukuru said. Justice Kayode glanced up at him, surprised. Hushed whispers spread through the courtroom. Dr Mara, who had half-risen and gathered his papers to leave the witness stand, sat down.

Bukuru stood up and drew a long breath.

'Dr Mara, how long have you practised as a psychiatrist?'

'Eighteen years,' answered Dr Mara in the even, unemotional voice of a man of science.

'And how old are you?'

'Forty-two next March.'

'Before you qualified as a psychiatrist, did you know any mad person?'

'Objection!' protested Okadi. 'What the witness did or knew before qualifying is irrelevant.'

Dr Mara and Bukuru paused, looking to the judge.

'Over-ruled,' said the judge.

'Yes,' the psychiatrist answered.

'Did you ever have time to closely observe the behaviour of this mad person?'

'Objection.'

'Over-ruled.'

'Yes.'

'Who was this mad person?'

'A man from my village.'

'He was born in your village?'

'Yes.'

'Was he mad from birth?'

'No. His condition manifested in his adolescence. One day he took to shrieking and dancing – especially at night.'

'Did he continue to live in the village?'

'Yes, sometimes at home but mostly at the marketplace.'

'Did he have relatives?'

'Yes, his widower father was still alive. And he had two brothers and a sister. Some cousins and so forth.'

'Did he still recognise them after he fell into, shall we say, a crazed state?'

'Yes, he often talked to them.'

'Tell us how he related to them.'

'He spoke to his father with appropriate reverence. At least

26

most of the time. When the old man died, he was at the funeral. As the oldest child, he threw the first earth into his father's grave.'

'Did he laugh at the funeral? Did he dance or ululate? Shriek or make other untoward noises?'

'No.'

'How would you describe his behaviour during the funeral?'

'Sombre. Sober. Restrained.'

'Like a normal bereaved person?'

'Yes.'

'Would you say then that there was a seeming suspension of his madness during the funeral?'

'Objection. The witness is being invited to speculate unnecessarily.'

Dr Mara and Bukuru again looked to Justice Kayode. He seemed to weigh the question for a moment.

'Sustained.'

'Let me rephrase the question,' Bukuru persisted. 'Did this madman appear during the funeral to – forgive the phrase – suffer a relapse into sanity?' There was suppressed laughter in the courtroom.

'He seemed to have a reprieve from his condition, yes,' answered the psychiatrist, removing his glasses and wiping, with the back of his hand, the sides of his eyes.

'How long did the funeral last?'

'Six days – that is the tradition.'

'What happened after the funeral?'

'He resumed his abnormal behaviour.'

'You mean his normal behaviour?'

There was another round of restrained laughter among the spectators. Even Justice Kayode bit his upper lip to keep from laughing.

The psychiatrist answered, 'You could put it that way.'

'Could you tell the court the oddest thing you ever saw this madman do?'

'Objection. The court's time is wasted by the accused asking the witness to tell unnecessary stories.'

Pause.

'Over-ruled.'

'I once saw him speaking to two ants in a threatening way.'

'Go on.'

'Apparently he'd been stung by an ant as he slept. Later on he came upon two ants going about their business. "Stop!" he said to the ants. "I want to know which of you stung me in my anus while I slept under the baobab tree." The ants continued on their way. He addressed the faster ant. "Hey, you, stop! You appear strong-headed. Perhaps it was you who stung my anus. Confess and I'll let you free – only with a warning." The ant continued to move. So the madman brought down his big toe and flattened the ant. He then turned to the other ant and said, "Well, you've seen what happened to your headstrong brother. Now, stop and tell me, was it not he who stung my anus?" The ant continued to move. Again in anger the madman crushed the ant flat on the ground with his foot. That was the oddest thing I ever saw him do.'

The crowd in the courtroom chortled at the story. Bukuru stood straight-faced waiting for a return to order. Justice Kayode took a slurp of water, cleared his throat and asked whether Bukuru had exhausted his questions.

'No.'

'Proceed,' the judge commanded.

'Have you ever been stung by an ant?' Bukuru asked the witness.

'Yes, on a number of occasions.'

'Did you ever kill an ant on account of that?'

'Yes.'

'Were you sure in every instance that you had killed the ant that had stung you?'

'I can't say that I was. Not in every instance.'

'Is it right, then, to surmise that as far as ants go, you believe in retribution?'

'Objection. The question is irrelevant and frivolous.'

'Over-ruled.'

'I'm not sure I understand the question,' said the psychiatrist.

'You have no problem with killing an ant that has stung you?'

'No, I have no problem with that.'

'Nor do you have a problem with killing an innocent ant – one that hasn't stung you?'

'I don't think of ants as guilty or innocent,' answered the psychiatrist.

'But apparently your village madman was concerned with that principle, wasn't he? He was interested in finding out which ant was responsible for stinging his anus, wasn't he?'

'Apparently,' Dr Mara answered, with a confounded look.

'And he was apparently willing to forgive the quote and unquote "guilty" ant – if only he got a confession of guilt, wasn't he?'

'Apparently.'

'If you saw a man who went about killing every dog in sight simply because one dog had bitten him, would you consider his action sane?'

'Objection! This is an egregious abuse of the court's time and courtesy.'

'I don't see how,' retorted the Elephant. 'Over-ruled.'

'No.' Dr Mara wiped a trickle of sweat off his face, like one wiping tears.

'Returning to part of your earlier testimony, why do you think the madman remained restrained during his father's funeral?'

'Perhaps because his socialisation had become strong before the onset of his psychiatric symptomatology. Perhaps he remembered how people were expected to behave at funerals.'

'Perhaps, then, he had not been socialised about dealing with ants. Or perhaps that part of his socialisation had been weak, would you say?'

'Objection. This is argumentative. It's not a question but a tendentious suggestion.'

'Sustained.'

Bukuru stroked his chin. Dr Mara fiddled with the pile of files in front of him. A smile spread over Bukuru's face as, turning to the judge, he said, almost in a whisper, 'I have no more questions.'

Open laughter broke out in the courtroom as the psychiatrist descended from the stand. In his confusion he dropped a number of files and papers and knelt, flustered, to recover them.

'Easy does it, Dr Mara,' said Justice Kayode. 'Take your time.' The psychiatrist bared his teeth in a smile that seemed a mixture of apology, gratitude and self-pity.

The judge's gavel fell three times, conjuring silence. 'The court will recess until 3 p.m.'

Chapter Four

When the proceedings resumed, Lieutenant Lati took the stand as the prosecution's last witness.

'Identify yourself to the court.' Jerome Okadi spoke in a subdued voice.

'My name is John Lati. I head the homicide division at Madia police headquarters.'

'Before we address specific issues, do you have any general observations on this case you wish to share with the court?'

'Yes,' Lati answered. He cleared his throat deeply, then turned in the judge's direction. He stated that in his twenty-one-year career he had never investigated a case that baffled him more. Then, in a soliloquy, he asked a series of questions, answering each in turn.

'Did we find any motive for this homicide? No. Did we see any physical evidence that tied the accused to the prostitute's death? No. Is it unusual to find homicide cases without apparent motives? No. Do some people kill just for the sake of the thrill? Absolutely yes. Is the circumstantial evidence against the accused strong? Without a doubt.'

Mr Okadi nodded vigorously throughout this speech and paced the room, two steps in one direction, then two in another, his chin held up. He stabilised himself on one foot, then pirouetted to face Lati.

'On a scale of one to ten – ten being the strongest – how would you rate the circumstantial evidence?'

'Without a doubt, at ten.'

'Outline for the court, detective, the nature of this evidence,' the prosecutor urged.

'First of all, independent corroboration places the accused in the proximate area where the drowning death occurred. The lifeguard has testified that the accused was at the scene of death. Second, he admitted knowing that the deceased was a prostitute. He would not have been in possession of that information were he and the deceased not acquainted prior to her death. Third, he admitted under interrogation that the deceased drowned while running from him. He also revealed that she shrieked as she ran. People only run from danger, from those who have harmed them or are intent upon harming them. Fourth, the lifeguard on duty testified that the accused hindered the resuscitation of the deceased.'

'Is that all?' Okadi asked, with the confidence of a man aware that there was more.

'No. We also found the accused man's explanation of the woman's death highly suspect.'

'Could you explain to the court what you mean by suspect?'

'Yes. His account was implausible, full of holes.'

'Kindly describe them for the court.'

'Yes. The accused falsely claimed that the deceased was raped by a gang around 4 a.m. He said he couldn't see the faces of the attackers because it was too dark. He further claimed that the unknown assailants abandoned the deceased and left in a truck. He stated that one hour after the assault ceased, he approached the site of the assault to offer help to the victim. Then, according to him, she screamed with terror and ran into the waves.

'In the course of our extensive and thorough investigation we interviewed several vagrants who sleep less than two hundred metres from the spot where the deceased drowned. None of them had heard any screams around the time of the alleged gang rape – 4 a.m. But they were able to corroborate the suspect's story of a shriek closer to 7 a.m. – the estimated time of her death.'

'What conclusion did you draw from that?'

'That the accused spoke the truth only in admitting that the woman was running away from him at the time of her death.'

'Tell the court, Lieutenant. Did the accused make any other doubtful statements?'

'Yes, indeed. He claimed that he ran after the deceased to save her, but found her too afraid to be rescued.'

'Did your investigation find this to be true?'

'Absolutely not. In fact, the lifeguard indicated that the suspect hindered his effort to resuscitate the deceased.'

'Are there other falsehoods the court should know about?'

'Yes. The accused tried to malign the reputation of the Madian armed forces by claiming that the deceased was raped by soldiers, specifically members of the vice task force. He also falsely accused a member of the Armed Forces Revolutionary and Redemptive Council of being a rapist and murderer. He alleged that twenty-three years ago, this distinguished officer raped and killed a woman.'

'And your findings?'

'That the claims were totally baseless. We could not establish that soldiers were anywhere near B. Beach on New Year's Day. As for the accused's retrospective allegations against the member of the AFRRC, we could not find that such a prostitute ever lived, much less that she could have been raped or killed by the said officer, who is a venerable public servant.'

'Your testimony to the court, therefore – and correct me if I am wrong – is that the accused raped the deceased, a prostitute, and caused her death?'

'Yes, that is my testimony.'

'Then he invented an elaborate hoax to deflect attention from himself?'

'That's my testimony,' repeated Lati.

'And you are prepared to aver to the court that this testimony is truthful, that you arrived at your conclusions after an exhaustive, thorough and professional investigation?'

'Indeed, I am,' said the detective.

The prosecutor smiled. 'No more questions, Your Honour,' he said, slowly turning to the judge.

Lati stood up, bowed slightly to Justice Kayode and made to leave the witness box. Bukuru's raised hand caught the judge's attention.

'Yes. Do you wish to cross-examine the witness?'

'Yes, Your Honour. Yes.'

Justice Kayode made a gesture of assent. 'Good. You seem to have woken from slumber. The witness is all yours.'

A tense silence fell in the courtroom. Bukuru and the detective stared at each other, braced. Bukuru narrowed his eyes.

'You have wilfully lied here today, haven't you?'

'Objection, Your Honour!' shouted one of the prosecutors. 'The question has prejudicial intent.'

'Sustained!' Justice Kayode fixed Bukuru with a censorious eye. 'You may not use language that blatantly questions the integrity of a witness.'

'But he spent his entire testimony calling me a liar,' Bukuru protested.

'You're the accused in this case, not Lieutenant Lati. Now continue with the business of cross-examination.'

Bukuru ignored the order, addressing himself to the judge. 'But am I not also presumed innocent?'

'Don't let me run out of patience with you,' the judge warned. 'My court's time cannot be wasted. I said, and I say

34

again, for the last time: continue your examination of the witness.'

Bukuru turned towards Lati.

'How did you arrive at the conclusion that the statements I made were untrue?'

'Through our investigation.'

'How many people did you interview in the course of it?'

'Three.'

'And all three, I take it, are the so-called vagrants?'

'Yes.'

'Why didn't you talk to any members of the vice task force?'

'We found no cause to. We can't waste our time and other people's time on the basis of a suspect's false allegations.'

Bukuru looked towards Justice Kayode. The judge's face remained impassive.

'Nor did you talk to any of the prostitutes arrested by the vice task force?'

'No.'

Bukuru wiped his hand across his brow. 'The Head of State created the vice task force, I believe in September or October of last year. Do you remember what their mandate was?'

'Yes, to rid the city of prostitution. It's part of the effort to attract foreign tourists to the city.'

'Oh,' Bukuru said. 'I used to think prostitution helped tourism, that many tourists actively seek a bit of exotic native sex. Thanks to you, I now know better.'

Chuckles spread through the courtroom. Justice Kayode brought down the gavel on his desk and restored decorum. Bukuru faced the detective, grim.

'When he set up the task force, I believe His Excellency told the soldiers it was a declaration of war on prostitutes. Do people get wounded in a war?'

'Yes.'

'And killed?'

'Yes.'

'Why, then, do you find it hard to believe there would be casualties in a war declared by your commander-in-chief? You're not by any means implying that an officer of the calibre of General Isa Palat Bello doesn't know what he's talking about when he declares war?'

A look of exasperation came over the judge's face. 'The witness may not answer this question.' Disgustedly, he said to Bukuru, 'You must not talk about His Excellency with sarcastic levity. The patience of this court is not inexhaustible.'

'Your Honour, I was only trying to . . .'

'Don't Your Honour me,' the Elephant fumed. 'Just continue your cross-examination.'

Bukuru folded his hands in front of him and paced the room as Okadi had done. Suddenly stopping, he swept a glance in the direction of the reporters. His lips parted in a half-smile. Then he spun round on the witness.

'You're convinced, detective, that I raped and killed the deceased woman?'

'Yes, I am.'

'Not only that, you are convinced that I am a serial rapist and murderer?'

'Yes.'

'Is it fair to assume you read the newspapers two days ago?'

'Yes.'

'Did you see reports about another woman's corpse found on Coconut Beach?'

'Yes.' Lati looked uncomfortable. 'My department is investigating that incident.'

'Do you imagine that I somehow slipped out of detention and committed that crime?'

'It's the work of copycats, criminals inspired by your example.'

'Is it possible those criminals are soldiers?'

'Impossible.'

'Let's return to the crime I am charged with. Did I not tell you, detective, that the deceased was assaulted for at least two hours by members of the vice task force?'

'You did.'

'And that many other prostitutes were similarly raped? Indeed, that one such prostitute spoke to me?'

'You lied.'

'You have not answered my question.'

'You did, but it was a lie. The police have received no reports from any prostitute to the effect that members of the task force raped her.'

'Mr Lati,' Bukuru said, pronouncing the detective's name as one might a profane word. 'How many men did the police prosecute last year for rape?'

The detective said nothing.

'Answer my question, detective.'

'I don't have the figures handy,' said the detective.

'Ten?'

'Maybe.'

'But maybe not?'

'Perhaps.'

'Is it possible that there was not a single prosecution for rape?'

'Yes. There are years in which we receive no reports of rape.'

'Would it be because women never get raped in this country?'

'Objection!' came a voice from the prosecution bench. 'The witness is being badgered with irrelevant questions.'

Bukuru looked at the judge. 'My point is to show that women

hardly report rape cases to the police. The police cover up assaults on women. I *know*.'

Justice Kayode had a doubtful air. 'What you think you know is irrelevant. I'm afraid the police cannot be put on trial here. The objection is sustained.'

Bukuru shook his head despairingly, then resumed his questioning.

'You told the court that I tried to implicate a – to quote you – powerful member of the military government as a rapist and murderer.'

'That's correct.'

'I believe I told you that the woman in question was a prostitute. That the same officer murdered her about a year later. Right?'

'Right.'

'Mr Lati, could you tell the court who General Isa Palat Bello is?'

'Objection!' shouted the two prosecutors in unison.

Justice Kayode fixed Bukuru with blazing eyes that seemed to burrow into him.

'Listen to me, Mr Man of No Name! You must understand and respect due process in this court. This is a court of law, not a civics class. I'm sure that everybody in this room' – he pointed to a pregnant woman among the spectators – 'everybody, including the baby in that woman's womb, knows that General I. P. Bello is the president and commander-in-chief of the Madian armed forces. Your question is grossly improper. It is a blatant and wilful show of disrespect to the person and office of His Excellency, the Life President of the Sovereign Republic of Madia. Let me sound a strong warning, once and for all: this court will not sit idly by and allow you to use the name of His Excellency in vain! I have already tolerated too much of your madness.'

His fierceness spent on this tirade, he added, 'Objection sustained.'

'Detective Lati,' Bukuru continued, 'did I not tell you that twenty-three years ago, General Isa Palat Bello raped a woman named Iyese?'

'Objection! This is insufferable!' exclaimed the junior prosecutor.

'Sustained!' thundered the Elephant.

A fearful stillness pervaded the courtroom. One spectator let out a nervous cough; others murmured. The judge sat back in his chair, poised between rage and resignation.

Bukuru pressed on. 'Did I not tell you, Mr Lati, that this woman was eventually murdered by Isa Palat Bello?'

The courtroom erupted into rowdy disorder which even Justice Kayode was powerless to suppress.

'Objection! Stop the madness!' cried the junior prosecutor, running towards the judge's bench.

'Order! I rule the accused in contempt!' pronounced Justice Kayode, bringing down his gavel with deafening force.

Detective Lati descended shakily from the witness stand. On the courtroom floor, four detectives fell upon Bukuru from behind and fastened handcuffs on him. The mayhem in the courtroom increased as many spectators pressed for a glimpse of the trapped man.

The Elephant rose to his full height. His gavel struck discordant notes, out of sync with his repeated cries of 'Order! Order!' Gradually the din died down. Justice Kayode waited for complete silence.

'The court hereby recesses for fifteen minutes,' he said in a hoarse voice. Mopping his brow, he walked away.

When the judge returned to the courtroom, twenty minutes late, the expression on his face showed that he had recovered his strength. He let his gaze fall on Bukuru, who sat between two policemen, shackled.

'In all my years as a judge I have never before seen such a blatant display of malicious contempt as took place today. My first instinct was to sentence you to jail for eternity – lock you up and throw the key into the Atlantic! – as a lesson that you cannot come to court and scandalise the good name and immaculate reputation of His Excellency.

'But – because this is a court of law, not a court of vengeance – I have tempered justice with mercy in arriving at the following rulings:

'(1) The members of the press are barred from reporting any part of today's proceedings where the good name of His Excellency was maliciously smeared. Any reporter who flouts this order will be summarily dealt with.

'(2) I shall appoint another psychiatrist to evaluate the defendant's mental state and report his findings to the court. After the depravity we all witnessed today, it is my considered opinion that a second psychiatric opinion is called for.

'(3) In order to allow ample time for the new evaluation, this case will be adjourned for two months, until 15 March at 9:30 a.m.'

The judge's gavel traced an arc as it came down one last time – *koi!* – on the varnished wooden bench. As the spectators began to file out of the courtroom, there was something disappointed about their gait – as if an exciting performance had been interrupted as it hurtled towards its climax.

Chapter Five

'Your report is riddled with irrelevant details,' the news editor criticised, his face dour. Then, as my spirits sank, he brightened up: 'But, oh, so bold! This will earn you a file at the State Security Agency. Perhaps even a visit. Be prepared!'

For four days after my story's publication my nerves were set on edge. I shuddered whenever a human shadow approached me from behind and trembled when I heard an unfamiliar voice.

On the fifth day I awoke to the discovery that the nervousness had vanished. Strangely, I missed it. While it lasted, it had imbued my life with meaning and purpose, a sense of being in the dark swirl of events, in danger. The story, with its rich details of the courtroom drama, had made me an enemy of the state, an object of interest to the dreaded security apparatus. When nothing came of it and my life went on much as before, I felt that time passed dully, purposelessly. Other assignments seemed poor distractions. I could come alive again only when the trial resumed. Until then, there was little to do except count the days.

The ninth day after the adjournment, I was set to go home after a dull day spent covering a trade fair when a call came through from the switchboard.

'The caller says it's urgent,' the operator said to me.

I put the receiver to my ear, expecting an animated voice. Instead, the caller spoke in a carefully calibrated tone.

'My name is Dr S. P. J. C. Mandi,' came the measured voice.

'Let me warn you that this call concerns a highly confidential issue.' Then he asked me to meet him the next day at 12:45 p.m. outside the gates of Bande maximum security prison. I was not to tell anybody about the meeting, he said. Not even, he stressed, my editor.

'It's essential that you are on time, Mr Adero. And please wear a jacket. A fairly good one, but not too fashionable.'

He must have anticipated that I wanted to say something, because he quickly cut in: 'Any questions you may have must wait till we meet tomorrow. I wish to stress, again, that punctuality is of the essence. And appearance. Goodbye, Mr Adero.' Then he rang off.

I was incensed by the caller's air of mystery. Who did he think he was, to order me to a secret meeting, even instruct me on how to dress, without offering the slightest hint of what it was all about? His calm, clinical voice added to my irritation. My thoughts were a formless whirl, torn between fear and an instinct for self-preservation on the one hand and a hunger for danger and recklessness on the other. In the end I decided to go. Even so, I wanted to be cautious. At the top of a sheet of paper I wrote, IN CASE I'M MISSING. I gave details of my conversation with the stranger, then put the note in my top drawer.

◆

I left home at 9:00 a.m. the next morning in a rented Peugeot, taking the expressway out of Langa. About two miles to the tollgate, I ran into jammed traffic, cars moving forward at tortoise pace, the drivers besieged by hawkers and beggars. It was not until 10:11 that I passed the tollbooths. The caller had said the trip would take no more than forty minutes once the city was behind me. I turned left, southbound, onto a minor road which, according to my directions, should terminate at Bande prison.

It was a bumpy, potholed, dusty road through a flat and sorrowful landscape. For a long time I drove alone. Then I spied, far in the distance, the hazy outlines of a glistening object. It crystallised into a vehicle, the first I had seen for many miles on this sullen stretch of road. As it swept past I saw a marking on its side: MADIA PRISON DEPARTMENT. I ran full tilt into the cloud of dust it raised; through the rearview mirror I saw it swallowed up in mine. The fear inside me grew.

Shortly afterwards the road detached itself from the parched, flat plain and climbed a hill. From the top I could see the prison. My eyes skimmed the series of squat structures enclosed within its high walls. The prison was surrounded by lush vegetation.

At 10:50 a.m. I manoeuvred the car into one of the parking spaces marked for visitors. A moat ringed the prison, and a bridge connected the two worlds this moat sundered. An iron gate secured the bridge from traffic. The notice on the gate was sombre: WARNING: PRISON VEHICLES ONLY BEYOND THIS POINT. There was a security post beside the gate, manned by two officers.

The prison's footpaths, however, were laid with raked gravel. Freshly painted stones dotted the edges, and beds and borders were planted with flowers that glowed in the sunlight: amaranth, zinnia, lantana, impatiens, African violet, bougainvillea, hibiscus, red roses, morning glory, sunflowers, Africa-never-dies. The carefully tended flowers diffused a heady perfume in the air.

◆

Bande maximum security prison was the brainchild of Askia Amin, our country's first prime minister. He had seen a model for it during an official visit to Latin America. Upon his return he signed an order for a replica to be built in a reclaimed swamp, in a location as remote from the bustle of life as possible. He had no wish for the intended inmates – his political enemies – to be reached by the familiar sounds of the human world. Such sounds could only be a distraction to men and women secluded in the prison to contemplate the truths of life.

A few weeks after the completion of the prison Isa Palat Bello led a group of junior officers to stage our country's first coup. Amin and many of his ministers became the prison's first inmates.

◆

As I waited in the car park for Dr Mandi I grew drowsy with the gathering heat. My head began to throb. I shut my eyes.

'Mr Adero, I presume?'

I awoke with a start. The man whose voice had roused me was bent over the open window of my car, his face level with mine. He was smiling, but I could not tell his smile apart from a snarl.

'Yes,' I said, belatedly – after he had already proffered his hand. 'Femi Adero.'

'S. P. J. C. Mandi. Pleased to meet you. I hope it wasn't too much trouble for you, at such short notice and with all the secretive circumstances.'

He paused, waiting, the smile steady.

'It was no trouble at all.'

'Excuse me, Mr Adero, if I ask you for some form of identification. Anything with your photograph. Perhaps you have your driver's licence handy, no?'

My heart beat fiercely and I could only stare at him.

'Sorry,' he said, 'but I cannot proceed until I'm sure you're the person I invited. It's important.'

I fumbled through my wallet for my driver's licence. He inspected it without taking it from my hand. Smiling again, he motioned me out of the car. He walked towards the bridge and I followed, a step behind. We had only taken a few strides when he stopped.

'You already know my name, but let me introduce myself formally. I am a psychiatrist with the Madia Military Hospital. I have been asked to provide a new evaluation of suspect number MTS 1646.' He noticed my bewildered expression. 'That's the name officialdom gives the man you name Bukuru in your newspaper.' He laughed quickly, then became business-like.

'The suspect asked me to arrange this meeting. I know why he wants to see you, but it's not my business to tell. If everything goes well, you will meet him in ten or so minutes and hear from the horse's mouth.

'My own concern is to make our visit hitch-free. I'm taking a great risk in playing facilitator. You must now listen carefully.'

Dr Mandi said he was going to introduce me to the prison superintendent as Dr A. F. Tijani, a psychiatrist attached to His Excellency's office. He would say that he had received a call that morning instructing that I should participate in the evaluation.

'Now all I want you to do,' he said, 'is to play your part well. Affect a distant demeanour. Act like a man who understands power. Be a little arrogant. A little, I stress. And, of course, humourless. Leave most of the talking to me. If you have to say anything, be brief. And remember to throw in one or two scientific terms. Not pretentious stuff, just standard fare: psychosis, schizophrenic malady, aggravated neurosis. Anything to befuddle the prison strongman.'

His face became severe as he sized me up. Did he see the perspiration on my forehead, my trembling legs?

'Let me also warn you beforehand, Mr Adero – I'm sorry, Dr Tijani,' he continued. 'You're going to see things inside the

45

prison that may shock you. But don't show that anything is new to you. Act like one who has seen everything, a man who is accustomed to the workings of power.'

We had reached the superintendent's office. Dr Mandi tapped on the door and without waiting for an answer twisted the knob and walked in. The superintendent's assistant gave us an indifferent look. Long thin strands of her braided hair fell over her eyes, which seemed dull with boredom. Her skin was sallow, daubed with black splotches, and a smell like that of rotten onion gave her away as a skin bleacher.

'Is your *oga* in?' asked Dr Mandi.

'Yes, sir.'

'Tell him Doctors Mandi and Tijani are here to see him.'

'I remember you from yesterday, sir,' she said, indicating Dr Mandi. 'Take a seat, gentlemen.' As she ran off to the inner office to announce us, Dr Mandi turned to me and flashed a wide satisfied smile.

◆

As we talked, the superintendent shifted in his seat, his eyes darting from Dr Mandi to me, back and forth. His office was clean, uncluttered. A grey filing cabinet. A standing fan that blew hot air across the room. A large bookshelf bearing only a copy of *The Prison Manual*. A dust-coated vase that held a bunch of plastic roses. Two desk trays marked by somebody in a fit of bad spelling, Pennding and Addrest.

After listening to Dr Mandi's account of the reasons for my presence the superintendent complained that he had not received any direct communication about me from His Excellency's office. Dr Mandi interrupted him with a high spurt of laughter.

'You should know the way of authority. The powers-that-be

46

hardly deign to communicate their will directly to lower servants.'

The superintendent seemed about to say something in reply, but Dr Mandi's derisory laughter had wilted his confidence. He rammed his fist on a desk ringer and the assistant poked her head into the room, the rest of her body tucked safely behind the door. He asked her to run, quick quick, and fetch Corporal Felix. Moments later the warder sprang into the room, looking guilty, like a miscreant child.

'Bloody malingerer, what took you so long?' the superintendent bore down on him. Corporal Felix began to explain that he had come right away, but the superintendent raised his large, powerful arm. The warder hushed up in mid-sentence.

'Take these gentlemen to 1646. Immediately, with double quick march!'

Corporal Felix jumped at the command – a show of obedience that brought a small smile to his boss's face.

◆

The prison compound was deadly quiet, bare and barren. Grass lay about the surface like sun-dried algae churned out by the sea. A criss-cross of concrete paths led to small detached buildings, each containing ten cell units. The cells were sunk in darkness. A horrible stench flowed out of each door we passed, the stink of unwashed bodies mingled with the foulness of things that come from within them: faeces, urine, vomit, blood.

My bladder was bursting. I asked Corporal Felix where the toilet was. He shook his head and told me there was no running water. He pointed me to a spot on the wall.

'Na there we warders dey pee. Even superintendent, na there him too dey pee.'

A swarm of flies buzzed around the greyish spot.

'Thanks, but I'd rather not,' I said.

We stopped outside the cell marked 1646. Corporal Felix unlocked the iron-barred door, then stepped aside to let us into the cell.

Bukuru stood, his back propped against the wall that faced the door. His eyes gazed vacantly, hard.

'Thank you, corporal,' Dr Mandi said to the warder. 'You must leave now. Evaluations are conducted in private.'

The warder slunk away.

Bukuru's hard eyes seemed to soften, but he remained silent.

'Meet Mr Adero,' Dr Mandi said to Bukuru. 'But he's known within these walls as Dr A. F. Tijani.'

Bukuru steered his eyes to me. 'Thank you for accepting my invitation. I liked the reports you wrote on my arrest and the trial.'

'Thank you.'

'You must wonder why I wanted to see you. It's simple. I wanted to ask you to be the voice for my story.'

Voice. *Voice?*

'I don't know the meaning of what you ask,' I said.

'My life's in grave danger. For what I said in court, a decision was made to poison me.' He glanced at Dr Mandi, who gave an absent-minded nod. 'The plan has been shelved for now, because somebody leaked the information to the foreign press. But I don't know what might happen in the future. Isa Palat Bello could become desperate.'

Mandi, without looking at us, nodded again.

'The doctor has been very kind. He's given me sheets of paper to write my story – to describe my journey to this terrible place. I wanted to entrust the story to your hands. You never know, one day it may become possible to make it public.'

He sought my eyes. 'Like you, I started out as a young man working for a newspaper. But I was weak: I never wanted to be touched by anything that quickened the heart or made the soul sweat. Now, when I wish to speak out, I have no way of making my voice heard – unless you will help me.'

I bore the weight of the two men's eyes in silence, unable to fasten on any response. Why carry another man's load? Especially under the circumstances, when I could not tell how profusely it would make my own soul sweat.

'I know I have asked a difficult thing,' he said, reading my thoughts. 'But put yourself in my place. What choice do I have? This is a vicious fight, and I'm the underdog.'

Under the beseeching pressure of his gaze, I broke out shrilly, 'I, too, know how it feels to be an underdog.'

I fought back the temptation to sketch for them the dreary facts of my own life. The day the mask I took for my true face was torn away, making me a mystery to myself. The terrible way I found out, at twelve, that I was an adopted child. The fruitless search for my biological parents. How, only a year ago, my girlfriend had deserted me, giving as her reason her parents' discomfort with a suitor who was unaware of the source of his genes.

Bukuru and Dr Mandi waited in silence. Would I extend a helping hand to one of the losers in the brutal game of life? I had to: I could not turn my back on him.

Bukuru said he would finish writing in a matter of days, at most a week. We agreed that Dr Mandi would deliver the story to my home. In the guise of Dr A. F. Tijani, psychiatrist, I could come back to see Bukuru if I had any questions.

'Why have you become involved in this dangerous scheme?' I asked Dr Mandi as we walked to our cars.

He halted and raised his head to scan the sky. Then he sighed and his gaze came down, revealing eyes that had misted over.

'You and Bukuru both spoke of yourselves as underdogs. Well, I have known my share of troubles too. If you knew what they were, you might say that I have been the greatest underdog of all. But that's another story.'

I extended my hand. 'Here's to the adventure of three under-dogs, then. Goodbye.'

PART TWO

Memories

Dear Femi,

Your visit in the doctor's company lifted my spirits more than I can express in words. In this grim cell where I spend my days and nights, I count my blessings in the coin of such moments.

In your hands now lies the possibility of my salvation or damnation. I live an unprotected life, with nothing to deflect what the world throws at me. No shock absorbers. Everything hits me in the raw, leaves a sore.

It hardly matters that yesterday, through the peep hole in my cell, I saw the sun rise and saw it set. Whether I will again behold this simple magic of nature today and tomorrow is a question other men will decide.

I send you this, my story, neither with joy nor triumph but with a sense of relief. There were times, writing it, when I was racked by doubt. How could I make sense of things happening to me today by speaking of things that happened so long ago? How could I prod my tongue to uncoil and learn to speak again?

I can't even say I fully understand my own motives in writing this story. Is it a desperate way of clinging on to a life that lost its salt many years ago? Or a way of confessing my sins to myself, forgiving myself? Once upon a time I would not have been able to tell this story without first being at peace with my motives. I would have agonised endlessly, the narrative dead in my hand. Alas, I no longer have that luxury. Even if my motives are self-serving I think there is still some good in relating these events. I am not afraid to admit it: the story is flawed, as I am flawed. But it is the story I have to tell.

And yet, I'd like to believe that I have written these words for worthier reasons. I hope I have written not just to save myself, not just to raise my finger and point it at another man (for how could a sinner like me accuse another?), but to examine where my life has intersected with our wider history, how I have touched larger events and been touched in return. I want to reckon up my journey and Madia's, to calculate the cost of things done and things left undone.

Against the power of the state, I can only throw this story. I know: it is a feeble weapon. But it is the only weapon I have. A time shall come when those who today sit on the heads of others will themselves be called to account.

Chapter Six

Their eyes burrowed into mine, six eyes pretending to seek the truth. The voices I had collected over the many years of solitude crowded my head. They filled me with suspicion and distrust. Then one voice echoed clearly across space and time. 'Remember,' it warned, 'a story never forgives silence. Speech is the mouth's debt to a story.'

My grandmother had first spoken those words to me, days after we buried my father. A shame I did not understand her then, for I would not today be in this tragic puzzle that becomes messier the harder I try to disentangle its knots.

The trouble began the moment I told the detectives I knew who raped the dead woman. Okoro fished out his notebook and held a pen to it with eager readiness.

'She was raped, you said,' he said. 'How did you know that?' He began to scribble even before I spoke.

I spoke without reluctance. I narrated the vivid details of the two-hour assault, the woman's screams that had started just after 4 a.m., the male voices that tried to hush her up, the kicking and slapping that, finally, silenced her. I told the detectives how the men gathered themselves and went away, leaving the woman behind. How, a short while later, I searched for her through the dawn mist, following her sounds until I discovered where she lay. I told them about her low disgusted groans, her deathly panting. Then how, as I knelt beside her and spoke, she panicked.

'How were you able to determine the time of the assault?' Okoro asked.

'The bell at St Gregory's. It had just rung four times before I heard the screams. It rang six times just as her attackers were leaving.'

'You said earlier that you attempted to save her. How did she come to drown?'

'She panicked when she heard my voice. Then she bolted up and ran into the waves, shrieking all the way.'

'And what was she saying as she ran?'

'I couldn't catch her exact words, but she seemed to be pleading and cursing at the same time.'

'Can you tell with certainty how many men raped her?' Lati asked.

'Not exactly. It was too dark when it all started. But the street lights illuminated the figures as they left. I certainly counted as many as six men. There may have been more, I can't be certain. The mist was quite thick and I was at a distance. They left in a truck.'

'What kind?'

'A military truck.'

A shocked consternation came over the detectives' faces. 'What does that mean?' Musa snapped.

'The men were soldiers,' I said. 'Members of the vice task force. They wore military fatigues.'

'What madness!' Lati blurted out.

'What are you suggesting?' Musa asked.

'The rapists were soldiers,' I said. 'As I told you, men of the vice task force.'

'You can't accuse soldiers falsely!' Lati said sternly.

'You can be shot dead for that!' chimed Okoro.

In as defiant a tone as I could muster, I asked, 'Are you saying that the rapists were not soldiers? I saw them. And it was not the first time they raped women here. I even talked to one of their victims. Tay Tay is her name.'

The detectives glowered at me. Suddenly, Lati gave a laugh that was more a menacing flash of his teeth.

'Let me tell you something, my friend. We are not here to joke around with you. This is New Year's Day. I would rather be at home with my wife and kids. Or with friends eating and drinking. Instead, I am at work because a woman is dead. Death is our business and we don't joke with it. You just admitted you were the last person to see the woman alive. That's a serious issue. If I were you, I would not be joking around. Or making ludicrous statements.'

'Let me restate the point,' I said. 'The men who assaulted this woman were soldiers. I saw their uniforms and their truck. Last night was not the first time they raped women here. As I said, I actually . . .'

'Shut your mouth or I'll shut it for you!' growled Okoro. He took a step towards me, as though ready to strike me. I cast him a quick look and said, 'Isa Palat Bello is also a rapist and murderer.'

The detectives shook with nervous rage. 'Who are you talking about?' asked Okoro.

'The Head of State. He raped a woman I knew. Her name was Iyese. Later he killed her. She, too, was a prostitute.'

Lati's hand went to the gun secured on his waist. For a moment, my body stiffened. Then it relaxed again, ready for anything. Lati looked about him. The crowd's presence seemed to irritate him. Slowly, he unclenched his fist.

'You cannot besmirch His Excellency's name. We can summarily execute you. Enough of your nonsense. We're here to do a very serious investigation. Would you describe the drowning as suicide?'

'No. She probably thought I was one of the soldiers who raped her.'

'Did you know the deceased by name?'

'No.'

'Did the deceased know your name?'

'No, she was a total stranger.'

'Describe for us in full how she died.'

'I have already told you. It began with a scream. Then she ran into the waves.'

'She ran,' echoed Musa. 'Would you say you chased her?'

'Only to save her. I stopped when I realised she was too scared to be saved.'

'Would you say you aided her death?' he asked.

'No. The soldiers did.'

'Did you hinder it?'

'Her death?'

'Yes.'

'How could I? There wasn't much I could do. I tried to save her. And now I'm helping you to discover what happened to her. That's all I can do.'

'I wish to inform you that you're a suspect in this death. In the name of the state I demand your name.' A hardness had crept into John Lati's voice and face.

I said, 'Secret. Exile. Bubble. Void. I have many names.'

'Book him as Mr X,' Lati ordered his subordinates.

'That's used only for unidentified male corpses,' Musa reminded him.

'Do as I ask you!' Lati thundered. His anger was now on the surface, thick.

'Okoro.'

'Yes sir?'

'Handcuff the suspect.'

'Yes sir!'

Okoro approached with metal manacles. I then offered up my

58

hands. The handcuffs clanged shut around my wrists. Their steely iciness made me wince.

◆

Until I found myself in an unmarked police car, handcuffed, I had never really examined the dishevelled life I led as an exile. Indeed, as my years on B. Beach stretched out, it had come to seem as if the most important detour in my life had taken place in a vast vacuum, outside the regimen of time and space.

The stink of my body filled the car, repellent even to my nostrils. I remembered a favourite saying of my grandmother's: 'The odour that makes a man want to run away from himself carries death.'

The detectives drew up their noses, their lips zipped tight. Gazing at the manacles around my wrists, I suppressed the urge to laugh. What use was there in startling the detectives with the cry of a soul that, looking inward, saw much that was rotten and dead? Would they make sense of the journey that had taken me from the editorial board of a newspaper to their car? Was there a way in the world, or a language, to make them understand that my body had not always given off this repugnant smell?

The voice of my grandmother seemed to rise from deep within me. It again urged me to open up to the detectives, to unburden everything to them. Everything about my past and my present, about Iyese and Tay Tay and the common thread that linked them. Speak to them, her voice persuaded, about the shrieks that rent the air night after night. But they won't listen, I argued back to this voice. Even so, the voice insisted, describe everything in a way that will defeat their doubts.

◆

Five detectives joined Lati's team at the interrogation unit, a wide, high-ceilinged room, bare save for a circle of seats round an uncushioned swivel stool that was fixed to the concrete floor. I was made to sit on this stool. The eight officers formed a ring around me, like a pack of famished hyenas entrapping a prey.

'We want nothing but the truth,' one of them said as the interrogation began. It was a high-pitched male voice, from behind me. 'No beating about the bush. No rigmaroles. Now, how did you get the woman to the beach?'

I swung around on the chair, but saw, not one, but three stony faces.

'I didn't get her to the beach. The soldiers did.'

'Did she come on her own?' the same voice asked. This time I saw him, a dark big man.

'Soldiers brought her to the beach.'

'What do you have against prostitutes?' asked the only female interrogator. I spun around and faced her. Her lipstick was liquid and deep-red. It gave the impression of a mouth dripping blood.

'Nothing.'

'So why did you rape and kill them?'

'I didn't rape anybody. The members of the vice task force did.'

'You were caught redhanded. If you confess, you make things easier.'

'Nobody caught me at anything. I've tried to help your investigators with the truth.'

For three hours they took turns asking the same questions, until an awful pain throbbed in my unsupported lower back. Fissuring, this pain moved in two directions: one branch of it crept down my legs, the other spread upwards to my shoulders.

My neck was knotted into a taut hardness. I sat still, tracking the geography of the pain.

One interrogator cleared his throat.

'How many times did you rape her?' It was Musa.

Desperately I began to retell the whole story, but this time my narrative was incoherent, jumping and tumbling in time and space.

Suddenly Mr Lati shouted, 'Stop the crap!' I stuttered and stopped. 'We are not here to listen to your petty fancies. All we want to know is how you raped and killed the woman!'

His small obdurate eyes bored into me, the eyes of a man who would only see things one way.

I made a last appeal to be believed. 'I'm telling you the truth. I really want to help.'

He hissed disgustedly. 'This nonsense has made me hungry. Let's take a lunch break.'

The eight interrogators rose and filed out of the room.

◆

'We know an easy way to get the facts out of you,' said the woman when the session resumed. 'So, it's up to you.'

My back seethed with pain. My body already felt like a thing less alive than slowly dying and the suggestion of torture reached me only in a distant, abstract way.

'What do you expect of me?'

'The truth,' answered one of the interrogators.

'That's what I've been telling you,' I said.

The futile seesaw continued for the next two hours. Then Lati said, 'That's it for today. He's one of those who want to be tortured, but he can't stand much. Let's just give him the mosquito treatment.'

Two big-bodied guards marched into the room. They took hold of my arms and dragged me to a cell at the back of the headquarters. The cell was dim and dank, its air warm with unflushed faeces. As I entered, cockroaches scurried and disappeared under the mattress. A swarm of mosquitoes detached themselves from the walls and advanced on me like soldiers closing in on an unarmed target.

Night fell in that cell long before it did outside. In the deep darkness the mosquitoes attacked me in waves. I swatted at them until my arms became numb. Furtive roaches found my unshod feet. As they scampered away, I brought my heels down and squished them. *Pup! pup!* came the sound of their stomachs popping open, reaming out their entrails.

In the morning a police officer brought my breakfast. In the dim light as he opened the door, I saw a busy line of ants feasting heartily on the lifeless roaches. The mosquitoes had withdrawn to their perches on the walls, their bodies bloated. When I squashed them they squirted my own dark-red blood. The litter of dead things took away my appetite. Eventually the cell door was opened again. Two guards came in.

'You're wanted for interrogation,' one of them said.

They hoisted me up and propelled me out into the light. The ensuing interrogation was a relief from the smell of my cell, from the repulsive intimacy of roaches, bedbugs and mosquitoes. With each session the tension sharpened. My inquisitors were desperate for something other than the truth. Dismay was written on their faces. Their speech became snappy.

'Apparently you don't realise just how serious your situation is,' one of the officers sneered at the end of a gruelling session. 'Perhaps you should read what the papers have to say about your case.'

He thrust a copy of the government-run *Sentinel* at me. Back in my dim cell, I pored over it. I was not surprised to see that even though another prostitute had been attacked since my arrest, a guilty verdict against me was presented as a foregone conclusion.

'Well,' the officer began at my next interrogation, 'did the newspaper persuade of the need to tell the truth?'

'I have been telling the truth all along,' was all that I could say.

After the fourth day they announced that they had had enough of my 'lack of cooperation'. I was returned to my cell and left there, day and night, for forty-eight hours, until two guards came and took me away to the interrogation centre. A lone man waited there, a pair of glasses balanced on the end of his nose.

'Dr Mara,' he said cryptically after I sat down. 'A psychiatrist.'

He removed his glasses and began to fiddle with them, his eyes fixed on me. Then he took out a white handkerchief and began to polish the glasses, bringing to the act deliberate poise and indifference.

'Is it a good thing to rape women?' he began, as if addressing a moral question to himself.

'No,' I answered.

'How about killing? Is it excusable to kill?'

'No.'

'Would you consider a serial rapist a bad person?'

'Yes.'

'Always?'

'Yes.'

'Would it make a difference to you if such a person raped prostitutes?'

'No.'

'If you somehow raped a woman, would you see yourself as a bad person?'

'I didn't rape any woman.'

'But just for the sake of argument, let's say . . .'

I interrupted: 'I won't let you say a falsehood for the sake of argument.'

He slipped his glasses on and threw his head back, glancing up to the ceiling. He asked, 'Do you always obtain a woman's consent prior to having sex with her?'

'Sex has not been a part of my life for a long time.'

'But do you recall ever having sex with a woman without obtaining her unambiguous consent?'

'What's the purpose of the question?'

'I'm a psychiatrist,' he said.

'I know that. But what do you think *I* am?'

'I haven't found out yet.'

'And you never will.'

He smiled the smile of a man too self-assured to let my anger touch him. Then he asked, 'Could we talk about the woman who died on the beach on New Year's Day?'

In a dry tone I said, 'Yes.'

◆

In all, Dr Mara interviewed me over three days. On the second day I decided to test the possibility of winning his attention – not as a scientist, but as a human being. So I began to tell him about Tay Tay, the prostitute I had spoken to after she and two of her friends had been raped. For a moment he appeared to be engaged by the story. Then he lifted his hand, compelling me to stop.

'I am interested only in the questions I raise myself,' he said. 'Let's keep it that way, if you don't mind.'

After that he grew more and more remote, in what was clearly to him an impersonal search for a truth supported by evidence.

Like a pre-programmed machine, he rattled on, each of his unanswered questions followed by the briefest pause, then the next question.

In the end, despite my refusal to budge, he said, in a tone that revealed no frustration, 'That's all the questions I have. Thank you.' As he left the room even his steps were measured, as if scientific precision had permeated every facet of his life.

◆

The anger aroused in me by those sessions was still fresh as I cross-examined Dr Mara in court. I wanted to pummel him with questions that would force him to drop his mask of scientific objectivity and expose his human face, or what was left of it. I warmed with joy when he began to sweat on the stand and could have cried out in exultation when he dropped his files.

Chapter Seven

The sense of elation I had experienced in the courtroom dissipated as soon as the Black Maria drove through the gate of Bande maximum security prison where Justice Kayode had ordered me remanded until my trial resumed. The vehicle screeched to a halt inside the prison grounds and the warders ran about in a great bluster, as if my arrival as their ward was an event bound to shake the vital centre of their lives.

Alighting from the vehicle, I noticed the severity of the prison's design, the maze of concrete pathways that connected the cells. Tall mahogany trees stood outside the prison's high spiked walls, like spies.

Alone in a cell my heart shrivelled within me. The cell reeked of a variety of smells, mementoes left by all the previous occupants. The four walls seemed to draw imperceptibly closer, threatening in time to meet in an embrace and crush me. Death entered and stayed in my thoughts.

A beam of light shot through the cell's high-set window into the centre of the room. A multitude of motes danced within the beam, floating in a kind of hopeless limbo. I soon had the sensation of becoming one of the motes, freckly, weightless and flimsy, one among a million gyrators in an unending dance.

At night different sounds intruded on my solitude: the swaying of trees, the chirr of insects, the croaking of frogs, the shabby shuffle of roaches, the low requiem of mosquitoes and the terrible braying of demented prisoners.

♦

Eight days later I was visited by the new court-appointed psychiatrist.

Joshua was on duty that afternoon, a stocky fellow with a beer belly, a scarred face and small, serpent-like eyes. The other warders know to keep their distance, allowing me some space. They announce their presence discreetly, as if their eyes dread the prospect of meeting mine. Even when they bring me the bland-tasting beans that are the staple diet here, they shy away from my gaze. Joshua is different, a creepy monster with a surly coldness about him.

'S. P. J. C. Mandi,' I heard a male voice say outside my cell. 'State certified psychiatrist. I'm here on the orders of a high court to see suspect number MTS 1646.'

'De suspect dey sleep,' Joshua announced in his baritone.

'Well, then, we'll go in and wake him.'

'Go in?' asked Joshua incredulously. 'Go in? Mister doctor, nobody fit enter that cell. The man be crazy man. You can't fit to enter the cell. God forbid bad thing!'

'I'm the only one who can determine that the suspect is crazy. Not you, I'm afraid.'

'Don't fear, Mister doctor. I no do your job. But I get two eyes. I done look the man well, well. I swear, he be proper crazy man. Allah!'

'I'm awfully sorry then that Justice Kayode did not have the wisdom to appoint you. What's your name by the way?'

'Joshua,' answered the warder. 'Corporal Joshua.'

'Yes, Corporal Joshua. I happen to be the one asked by the court to report on the suspect's mental state. Now if you don't mind, could you please open the cell so that I may get to work?'

'I know say me no go school, but no way I fit open that cell. I no fit contravene protocol, at all at all.'

'Okay, Corporal Joshua, I see that we're a little confused here. My job is to interview the suspect – where and when I choose to do it. Your job is to provide me with security. And even then you must not be too intrusive. Do you understand?'

'I understand, but . . .'

'No, there are no more buts. You'll do what I ask. Now open the cell.'

Joshua grunted in capitulation and slid the key into the lock. In stepped a tall man, spare and athletic, bearded. He looked straight into my eyes and smiled.

'Dr S. P. J. C. Mandi,' he said, extending his hand for a shake. I sat up on my mattress and took his hand. He tightened his grip and held on for an oddly long time. 'It's a pleasure to meet you. A real pleasure.'

He was warm and suave, a man capable of establishing instant familiarity. I had to be on my guard, I cautioned myself; I had to keep unthawed some of my distrust of men who serve systems.

Finally letting go of my hand, he explained his presence. 'Justice Kayode has asked me to examine you.' He paused and averted his eyes, ashamed of the indelicacy of his words. 'Examine is perhaps not the right term. It's more like an interaction, a, what's the word I'm looking for . . . a dialogue. My job is to have a dialogue with you. Then to advise the court on certain matters.'

I nodded and he continued.

'Perhaps we should start by taking care of one or two procedural issues. The first is that I propose for our dialogue to be held right here, if you don't mind.'

69

I didn't, I told him, but where was he going to sit? Apart from a mattress on the floor the cell was bare.

'No problem at all. I intend to stand.'

I shrugged, indifferent.

'And, if you don't mind, may I request that you stand when we talk? Things are easier that way.'

'How?' I asked, hardly able to hide my curiosity.

'Blood circulates better when we stand. And people are more honest on their feet.'

'Are they? I know people who've told the baldest lies standing.'

In a serious vein, he said, 'It's a matter I've given serious consideration. And my conclusion is, it's harder to hide or distort our true feelings while standing.'

'Is this a scientific insight?'

'Call it my personal insight. No scientific journal would be likely to accept an article from me on the subject. But who cares? Some of the most important discoveries in life have never been reported in any journal.' He winked at me, a twinkle in his eye. 'You may be interested to know that some of my colleagues view me as something of a maverick. The unkinder ones might even call me a quack.'

Disarming and charming as he was, I had to remind myself sternly that he was not my friend. He was a scientist, I a caged animal in his laboratory. He might masquerade as a genial and humorous man but he could just as easily slip into his other skin as a diviner of minds. What was he here for but to plumb my deepest motives and uncover my hidden desires?

'I have no problem standing,' I said gruffly.

'Thank you.' His tone sounded a little officious. 'Now the second procedural matter has to do with the length of our meetings. You have the veto. You may call things off any time you wish.'

'Very generous of you, Dr Mandi.' I spoke too brightly.

'Ah, there's the issue of nomenclature to iron out. I'm quite happy with my initials. You must call me S.P.J.C.'

'That would be presumptuous. Besides, it's such a mouthful! Ess Pee Jay Cee.'

'Well, that's what you get when the Catholic Church names you. Simon Peter came with baptism. Jude with confirmation. My parents threw in Chika to appease the ancestors. For years I didn't know how to hold the names together. You don't walk up to people and introduce yourself as Simon Peter Jude Chika Mandi. Somebody might fall asleep while you're at it. But my chemistry teacher in secondary school solved the problem. He strung together the initials I have used ever since. Saved me a lot of headache, that wise fellow.'

I began to smile, until I saw the doctor's eyes fixed on my teeth. Was he puzzled by the brownish stain on the two front ones? I clamped my mouth shut.

'I understand that you absolutely refuse to tell anybody your name.'

'On the contrary,' I said in a low, weary voice. 'I do tell my name.'

He laughed. 'Like the ones you gave to the detectives? Those won't do. Nobody is going to put down Exile on an official document. Perhaps you should know that the prison bureaucracy hasn't given you a very flattering name.'

'You mean MTS 1646?'

He nodded.

'I've been wondering,' I said. 'What does it mean?'

'1646 is of course your cell number.'

'I figured that out. But MTS?'

'Mentally Troubled Suspect.' He scanned my face for my reaction. I averted my eyes, and shrugged. In a strange way I found the information laughable, like a fool's predictable witticism.

He fell silent, twittering. Then he said, 'I have to leave now.

71

We can't get into the big issues today. I'll return tomorrow at 1:30. Would you need anything?'

I thanked him, but said no, he could not give me what I wanted. Then I told him about the cockroaches and bed bugs, the mosquitoes and their sad songs.

'I can't claim to know much about roaches and bed bugs. Their history is as shrouded as their ways.' Then, moving slowly towards the door, he said, 'But there is a story about mosquitoes and the ear.'

'There *are* stories,' I corrected him. 'I know quite a few of them. But I still hate their melancholy droning.'

'You sound like a harsh critic.' He was now at the door. 'But remember that mosquitoes may be more moved by kindness.' He laughed, and without looking back, said, 'See you tomorrow.'

He exited so fusslessly that, moments later, I still felt his presence in the room, reinforced by the echo of his parting words: *moved by kindness, kindness, kindness.*

◆

I looked forward to my next meeting with Dr Mandi with mixed emotions. Expectancy was mingled with a sense of foreboding, a vague fear that peril lay in store if I placed too much trust in the psychiatrist.

He opened the conversation gravely. 'I've thought a lot about the way we ended yesterday: the bit about MTS.'

'Oh.' I was not sure what this was leading to.

'I *know* you're not mentally troubled.'

My brows shot up. Had I heard right?

'If you believe that, then the adjournment is a waste of everybody's time. Your report will merely repeat what Dr Mara has already told the court.'

'I'm afraid not. My hands are tied in that regard.' His face was mournful and tired.

In a perplexed tone I said, 'I don't get you.'

Dr Mandi narrowed the space between us, to within the range of quiet speech. 'The state, my friend, has decided to try you as a mad person. That's the only reason the case was adjourned. After what happened in court, you must understand why.'

'But I don't,' I protested.

'Don't you understand the implications of saying in open court that His Excellency is a rapist and murderer?'

'But that's the truth!' I cried, forgetting to subdue my voice.

The doctor's eyes danced in the direction of the door. I turned and saw Joshua watching us with alarm, the whistle between his lips. I said, 'It's true. These mosquitoes won't let me sleep.' Joshua removed the whistle, shook his head and scuffed away. After his disappearance, I faced the doctor and continued in a lower tone. 'What I said in court is the truth. The man is a rapist and murderer.'

Dr Mandi put his mouth close to my ear and whispered, 'Who in this country doesn't know that? Remember he has run our lives for two decades.'

'But I'm speaking quite literally,' I said on a note of protest. 'Even before he seized power he raped a woman I knew, a prostitute. He later killed her. Quite literally, I must repeat.'

'I *know*. And you know what?' A conspiratorial glint was in his eye. 'Most believe your story. It's the topic of conversation everywhere: here in this city, throughout the country, even overseas. The reports by the foreign media are what Bello's most concerned about: he's been trying to spruce up his regime's image. That's why you're in trouble. You can't publicise dirty secrets about the Life President and hope to sleep peacefully.'

I sighed bitterly. 'I realise that.'

'I have received clear orders from His Excellency's office to report that you're a madman. I was compelled to sign a paper to that effect.'

I threw him a disgusted look.

'I had little choice,' he said.

The anger that welled up inside me was of an odd kind, tinged with contempt and pity. As our eyes met again, I said, 'Whatever happened to principles? And integrity?'

He shrugged, less ashamed than I thought he should be. 'In the real world necessity sometimes takes precedence over conscience.'

'I pity any man who would say that!'

'I probably deserve pity. But I know it could have been worse. For both of us.'

'How?'

He again inclined himself forward, to whisper into my ears. I drew my head back, as though to avoid bad breath.

'You were to be poisoned,' he said. 'That was the first plan.'

He saw the startled look on my face and smiled, as if privy to still darker secrets.

'Yes, my friend, I hear things. I know a statement was already drafted to the effect that you committed suicide. Yes, that you recanted, then took your own life. That you couldn't live with the shame of the bare-faced lies you told in court. You owe your life to some anonymous fellow who published a letter in the international press to the effect that he could corroborate your allegations. He said he feared His Excellency would order you to be killed in order to cover up sordid facts in his past. The letter was published the very day your food was to be laced with enough cyanide to kill a cow. That's what forced the presidency to abandon its original idea and switch to Plan B – to discredit you. Which is where I come in.

'I was told what to do, at gunpoint. When your trial resumes, I'll take the stand and describe you as schizophrenic. Justice

Kayode will pronounce you guilty on one count of second-degree assault and one count of second-degree murder. Because of the international attention, the death penalty has been ruled out. You'll be sent to jail for a few years in the hope that the world will forget you and all you said in court. That's the idea.'

'That's the idea? And everybody knows it?'

'Well, let's say the major actors. Certainly Justice Kayode, the prosecutors, the police. A new decree will be issued tomorrow that makes mad people legally responsible for their crimes. The decree will be made retroactive, specifically to cover your case.'

More out of fury than doubt, I asked, 'Why should I believe you?'

'Good question. I don't know the answer.'

After a moment I asked, still agitated, 'If my fate is already sealed, then why are you here? Why is there a trial at all? The system you serve could have thrown me in jail without a trial. It happens every day. So why the needless ceremony? Why the adjournment?'

'The reason is called due process. This country is in deep trouble if Western diplomats send home reports to the effect that Madia doesn't observe due process in criminal trials. Or that we don't apply the rule of law. There's nothing worse than that to discourage foreign investors, freeze international aid, and keep the tourists away. The state may make up its mind behind closed doors but it must stage a public show to impress upon the world that it's an open, deliberative machine. Nor is Madia peculiar in this regard. It's the same everywhere: Europe, the United States. In your case Justice Kayode must go through the necessary motions even if he has reached a verdict *a priori*. Indeed, especially then.'

◆

Due process and the rule of law. The phrases resurrected a figure from years ago, a professor at the University of Madia who ran a course in Legal Ethics. He was a fattish man with restless eyes, popular with students for his unusual phrases and his classroom style. When he taught, he jumped and romped and beat up the air, like a novice karate artist in practice.

One day he strutted into class, wrote RULE OF LAW on the blackboard, and underlined the topic with a quick unsteady line. Then, making a sharp turn towards the class, he exclaimed, 'To hell with the rule of law! Give me the rule of justice!'

He was crazy, that was the consensus of his colleagues. They said a professor like him was the price the country paid for recruiting jeans-wearing, cursing, American-educated academics. Nobody disputed that he was a legend in his own right. One day at a faculty meeting he put his hand in his pocket for a piece of paper but pulled out a condom instead. He had done it in error, this much his detractors conceded, but he still had to be a lunatic to carry such things around.

Sam Ajira – that was the eccentric professor's name.

◆

'Do you know how I feel right now?' I said to Dr Mandi. 'Like a fly trapped in beer. Drowning more and more each time I bat my wings to leap to freedom.'

'Talk to me,' he said. 'Tell me your story.'

'You're part of this charade,' I snapped. 'I don't want to participate in it any more than I have already.'

'Trust me,' he said.

'Trust you? You who have signed a false report. You who will say things in court you know to be untrue. Trust you?'

Briefly, his professional composure seemed to unravel. 'A gun was put to my head. Yes, I could have chosen to die for integrity and principle. Sometimes, believe me, I feel ashamed that I didn't. But what principle does a dead man defend? What truth does he espouse? You may not know it now, but I'm also going out of my way to help you.'

'What exactly do you want from me?'

'Tell me everything that happened.'

'Why? I tried to tell the police and Dr Mara after my arrest, but they were not interested. I tried to tell it in court, but the system you serve stopped me.'

'The slaves of the system. That's who stopped you,' he said.

'But aren't you one of those slaves?'

'How can I deny it? But I'm an unhappy slave.'

'The only thing I'm left with in the world are memories. And I honestly don't trust you enough to share them.'

He scratched his head. Then he said, 'Do you know a fellow named Ashiki?' I trembled, but said nothing. 'Well,' the doctor continued, 'I haven't met him yet, but I believe he found out that I was working on your case. He left me a message to pass on to you.' He pulled a piece of paper from a file and handed it to me. The message was handwritten in capitals:

THE JOURNEY BEGAN AT GOOD LIFE

'A bewildering message,' the doctor suggested.

'Not to me,' I answered.

In silence, I thought about the implications of this development – the sudden exhumation of the one man who knew something about my previous existence.

'I'll tell you my story, under certain conditions,' I said. 'First, I want to write everything down. So I need pens and sheets of paper.'

He nodded his agreement and handed me a notebook and a pen to be going on with.

'I'd also like to see the *Daily Chronicle* reporter. I want him to be the custodian of my story.'

A frown crossed his face. 'It's impossible to smuggle a reporter in here.'

I shrugged. 'If you want me to tell my story . . .'

He smiled at my persistence. 'All right. Perhaps it will only be difficult, not impossible. I will try to arrange to bring him to you.'

'Thank you. Meanwhile let me write a message, just in case you see Ashiki.'

I tore out a sheet from the notebook and wrote, 'Violet made death easier to bear.' The feel of the paper brought back pleasures I had long forgotten, the scratchy song of pen and ink.

Chapter Eight

Until my arrest and that ride in the back of a police car, I had lived under the illusion that nothing was misshapen about my life. It was the world that had gone mad, not me. But after the departure of the psychiatrist I looked at myself with hard, unsparing eyes, determined to pinpoint the very moment when, renouncing everything that lay in my past, I took a strange turn on the road of life. The details of my alienness flowed like light into my eyes. It was there in the stink of my armpit, in my smutty fingernails, in my tangled-up beard and long shaggy hair.

I saw myself as a man who, forgetting where he started his journey, was condemned to wander for ever, without destination. Parts of myself lay in the mists of the past, lost. But which parts? How could I calculate what was lost when I could not say with any certainty how much of who I had been had survived?

My thoughts turned to Ashiki, the man Dr Mandi had mentioned. He and I had served together on the editorial board of the *Daily Monitor*. It was he who introduced me to Iyese. In all likelihood, he was also the anonymous source who saved my life, the man who alerted the foreign press to the fact that I was in danger of being poisoned. It would be just like Ashiki to step out of the shadows after all these years.

◆

How many years?

My mind went back to the day when I accepted a job at the *Daily Monitor*. It was in July of 1964. Two months earlier I had graduated from Madia University with a degree in Journalism. The *Monitor*, a small but popular newspaper based in Langa, hired me as deputy political editor, a title whittled down to the acronym DePe, embossed in black on a silvery plate that hung outside the door of my cramped office. By virtue of this post I was also a member of the paper's editorial board, six men and one woman who met three times a week to weigh the world's problems.

On 1 October 1960 our country had groped its way through the dark waters of the British womb and emerged into the world as a nation in its own right. The birth had been a long time coming. In 1884 representatives of British trading companies had taken to Berlin a map with which they persuaded their European siblings to acknowledge a large parcel of land on the western hump of Africa as a possession of the British crown. But the Berlin map of the new British protectorate concealed more than it revealed. It did not show, for example, that Madia contained more people than several European nations put together, or that these people spoke more than two hundred and fifty different languages, worshipped thousands of different gods and ranged in hue from the gradations of brown among the darker-skinned Bantu to the sepia of the much lighter groups of Semitic origin.

Through close to eighty years of colonial gestation the members of this protectorate (later to be called colony) learned to speak in the name of a political community that was new-fangled, strange and entirely of British conception. They demanded to be let alone to run their affairs as an independent nation. Some of their number who had mastered the whiteman's tongue and read his books that spoke from both sides of the mouth (extolling human freedom and liberty on the one hand, slavery and the notion of supremacy on the other) travelled to London to press their demand at a number of constitutional conferences.

British officials, who never thought of their colonial possessions as nations-in-rehearsal, turned up their noses at these natives in breeches speaking the civilised tongue in strange accents. But the English uppishness neither deterred the natives nor prevented the unravelling of the British Empire, an event accelerated by the world's second big war. In the end the Empire capitulated and Madia was proclaimed to the world as a newborn nation.

Newborn Madia was welcomed with a swell of hope and expectation. Many outsiders predicted that Madia would grow into a bright dynamic youth, one of the new nations likely to assume the mantle of world leadership in the twenty-first century. We Madians thrust out our chests and crowned ourselves the giant of the continent. There seemed to be good reason for our confidence. On the eve of British withdrawal, crude oil, this century's gold, had been discovered in Madia in vast reserves. We could dream, we assured ourselves, and transform our dreams into reality.

Instead, something went wrong early and never let up. The nation we inherited from the English was placed in the hands of politicians who sucked its blood until it became dry and anaemic. Overnight cabinet ministers puffed out protruding bellies they themselves called PP, for Power Paunch. What was left of Madia's swagger was a mere mask for impotence.

I read much of the history of Madia's birth in books designed to inspire pride and heroism. But I was also there, a minor actor and riveted observer, at the hour of our failure and disillusionment.

By the time I joined the *Monitor* in 1964 the political

upheaval that would ultimately blow up in the face of the government of Alhaji Askia Amin, first elected prime minister of independent Madia, had begun its slow build-up. The first minor crisis rocked the nation during my first week. The drama, which would be known as the Amanka-Yaw Affair (for its two principal actors), was a classic illustration of the government's tendency to go out of its way to shoot itself in the foot.

An obscure German magazine had published a photograph of Chief James Amanka, then the country's minister for External Affairs, dozing at a summit of the Organization of African Unity. The caption to the photo read, 'An African Minister's Rapt Attention'.

The story would have ended there had not Amanka convinced the prime minister to buy space in a number of local and European newspapers to denounce the magazine's 'malicious defamation'. The rebuttal backfired. A few days after its publication a British television company which had covered the summit aired footage of the minister in delirious sleep, his hands hugging his bulbous belly, his mouth agape.

Incensed, I wrote a column calling for the minister's resignation. From all over the country letters to the editor poured in in support of my call. Other newspapers, academics, labour unions, students and opposition politicians joined in. 'Resign or Be Fired,' shouted demonstrators, echoing the title of my article. Instead, the minister called 'a world press conference' at which he dismissed me as an imperialist stooge. On a different tack, he boasted that other African ministers did not exist as far as the international media were concerned, 'But when Honourable Chief James Amanka snores, the whole world pays attention!'

The protests intensified, forcing Prime Minister Askia Amin to reassign Amanka to the Ministry of Internal Affairs. Those of us who had wanted him dropped from the cabinet altogether continued our campaign, but our cause was eclipsed by the controversy that erupted over the surprise choice for the new minister for External Affairs.

Professor Sogon Yaw was at the time a political scientist at Madia University, a Marxist who detected a bourgeois plot in every imaginable event and situation. As a teacher, he cultivated a Marx-like beard and wore military fatigues that accorded well with his table-pounding, ranting style. Yaw's life was driven by one mission, he often said: to peel the mask off the faces of the enemies of the people, to expose local traitors and their foreign collaborators to public view.

Many of Yaw's fellow Marxists were shocked when his name was announced as Madia's new minister for External Affairs. They urged him to tell Amin to keep his capitalist bait. But they had underestimated the lure of power. Within a few hours Yaw presented himself to be sworn in. He arrived for the ceremony clean-shaven and made his vows in a quiet, even voice.

◆

I came to my post at the *Monitor* still under the influence of an idealism that had first captivated me when, as a youngster, I had overheard a discussion between two men in a village bar.

'After we chase away the British and regain our independence we're going to adopt communism as our operational ideology,' declared a bearded fellow nicknamed Man-Mountain Buzuuzu.

'What is this thing you call komanizim?' his companion, Iji, asked.

'Communism,' Buzuuzu corrected.

'What does it mean?'

'It means that people own everything in common,' explained Buzuuzu.

'Everything?'

'Everything.'

83

'Even houses?'

'Even houses.'

'So I can go to the chief's house and lie on his bed?'

'There will be no chief. Everybody is equal under communism.'

'I can go to a wealthy man and tell him that he is nothing more in this world than a fart?'

'Yes. But there are no wealthy men under communism.'

'There are not?' For a moment Iji's enthusiam seemed deflated. 'Komanizim means a lot of poor people, then?'

'You don't understand,' Buzuuzu said in a weary voice. 'Communism makes everybody wealthy. Nobody goes hungry. Poverty is swept away.'

'So if I'm hungry . . .'

'You can go to your neighbour's house and share his food.'

'I like it,' announced Iji. 'Where can people find this komanizim?'

'It was invented by a man called Karl Marx.'

'God will bless him.'

'There is no God in communism.'

'Really? No God?'

'No. The people are their own god.'

There was a lull in the conversation. Sipping their drinks, both men seemed to savour the promised sweetness. A moment later Iji turned to Buzuuzu.

'Let me ask you,' he said, his eyes shining with mischief. 'Can I go and fuck one of the chief's wives when you bring this komanizim?'

'No!' snapped Buzuuzu. 'Communism isn't about sex. Sex is decadent.'

Iji looked dejected. 'Leave the world as it is,' he said.

This conversation had made a great impression on the mind of the boy I was then, sent to the bar by my grandmother to collect her daily gourd of palmwine. By adulthood I knew that the seeming paradise of communal ownership was no more proof against wickedness and misery and horrible injustice than any other human political system, but I still nursed remnants of my early idealism in my heart.

My father was another reason I was thrilled about the job. My mother had died young. Thereafter my father, who was by all accounts a gifted broadcaster, had given up his budding career and taken a job as a teacher in order to be able to devote more time to bringing me up. Out of gratitude, when I went to university I decided to read journalism.

In my second year I was chosen to edit the departmental weekly newspaper. My father often wrote to me, offering criticisms and praise on my articles. Then in a letter that raised goose pimples all over my flesh, he assured me that my reputation as a print journalist was one day certain to surpass his as a broadcaster. I had hoped he would one day make the connection, that he would recognise my work in terms of his. But, coming too soon, the acknowledgement saddened me. My debt to him was much larger than his letter seemed to suggest.

My father's mother, Nne, also gave me cause for uneasiness when she foretold that I would achieve success and fame only if I washed my eyes in water, only if I was wise enough to avoid the misfortunes fate would put in my path. I had a dread of my grandmother. My father had told me many stories of her quirky wisdom, her habit of surprising people by divining their innermost thoughts, or their dreams, or foretelling events exactly as they would happen. The day her husband died she had begged him not to climb the particular palmtree from which he would have the fatal fall.

'Why are you speaking like a drunk this early in the day?' her husband had asked. The years he had lived with her had bred in him, not respect for her clairvoyance, but dismissive contempt.

'I saw in my dream a thing so terrible my mouth cannot speak it. That tree is bitter. You must sacrifice a cockerel to it to assuage its anger.'

Her husband had laughed her off. 'If that tree wants to eat a chicken, it must go to the market and buy itself one,' he said. One of his customers had ordered seven gourds of palmwine for a marriage ceremony, and my grandfather was not the kind of tapper to promise seven gourds without delivering.

When he set out that morning for his tapping rounds she followed him part of the way, admonishing in proverbs.

'The death that kills a puppy first blinds him. The headstrong who won't listen will finally obey the summons of the death mat. The housefly who has nobody to advise it follows the corpse into the grave.'

Her husband swaggered on in silence. Later that day, an old man returning from his farm heard muffled groans. Following the direction of the sound, he discovered my grandfather in a heap, blood surging from his mouth, dripping from his nostrils and seeping from his ears. The farmer ran to the village with a speed indifferent to the weariness of old bones. But when a small party arrived at the scene, my grandfather was already dead.

Chapter Nine

I waited until after my first day at work to write to my father with news of the job. It was the chattiest letter I had ever written him, and also the saddest. In it I described my first editorial board meeting.

Far from the solemn atmosphere I had expected, the meeting had shocked me with its frivolity. Most of those present quaffed brandy; the lone teetotaller drank cup after cup of tea. At the slightest opportunity the members abandoned serious issues in pursuit of trivial diversions.

The first such diversion occurred early in the meeting when someone used the word 'cocksure'. The only female member, a tall woman with low-cut hair, shouted, 'Point of order! I don't like any cocky words. Don't insert your cock in my discussion!'

Guffaws went out all around, inspired by the veiled lewdness of the woman's words. When they died down, the woman and two other members took turns relating more pointed prurient jokes revolving around the word 'cock'.

The most spirited baiting came from Soni, a sloe-eyed young man whom everybody called Mr Ways and Means. It was not long before I knew the meaning of the sobriquet. Whenever the editorial board members were unable, or unwilling, to dwell on a complex issue, they turned to Soni. He would take a moment as if in reflection, then utter his pat cliché: 'So so and so' – it could be the United Nations, the government of Madia, the

Medical Association or whoever – 'should find ways and means of solving the problem.'

The only board member who made serious comments and held himself aloof from the silliness was a man called Ashiki, whose bald head, as I wrote to my father, made him resemble a tortoise. His anguished detachment provided something to sweeten the bitterness of my general disappointment with the meeting. Also, I was curious to know how Ashiki managed to stand apart from his colleagues' foolish conduct, seemingly unperturbed. This Ashiki, I informed my father, was a man I intended to befriend.

◆

Several weeks after sending this letter to my father I had still received no reply. I sent another letter, express. Again, no response. I decided that something must be wrong at home. Perhaps with my grandmother, who had recently suffered a serious illness and virtually lost her sight.

I asked the editor for a week off. The next morning I took a taxi to Ido motor park and joined several other passengers on board a station wagon bound for Onitsha, a commercial town five hundred miles east of Langa.

My mood was nostalgic throughout the seven-hour journey. Memories of my father floated in and out of my mind. I recalled how he had set off my romance with words, how he had taught me words as sound long before I knew them as meaning. *Braggadocio. Hocus pocus. Tintinnabulation. Jiggery pokery. Brouhaha.* Words that were magical music to my ears.

The car arrived in Onitsha in the late afternoon. I completed my journey in a cab that ran the thirty-minute shuttle to my village. The driver dropped me off outside the bar in which years earlier I had listened to Man-Mountain Buzuuzu and Iji's conversation. Walking towards my home, I saw a woman sitting on a wooden ledge in the village square, head lifted to the sky. She called out my name. I started, then recognised my grandmother.

'Nne,' I addressed her. 'What are you doing here?'

'Watching the sun go home,' she answered.

'Watching the sun! Didn't father say . . .' I squelched the indelicate question.

'That I had gone blind? Why should weakness of sight stop me escorting the journeying sun?'

'I was surprised that you called out my name. How did you know it was me?'

'The scent of your spirit.'

'Scent? How does my spirit smell?'

She laughed, a high, full-hearted laughter. 'Just like your father's. A good smell.'

As we made our way home she said, 'Your father is waiting for you.'

'Waiting? But he doesn't know I'm coming.'

She laughed again. 'My son, you and your father carry the same blood in your bodies. He knows you are coming.'

She led the way, neither shuffling nor raising her legs with that exaggerated caution of the blind. Afraid that she might trip, I grabbed her hand. She wrested it free. 'You don't think I know my way?' she fumed.

'I don't know how you can.'

She jiggled a small dance. 'Don't kill yourself with anxiety, my son. The road takes care of its own. You don't understand because you've travelled too far from your hearth. You know what a big place the world is, but you have forgotten the language of your soil.'

I knew there was no use arguing with her. Not even my father, more skilled than I when it came to disputation, could match my grandmother. A story he once told me illustrated her dominance over him.

Five years after my parents' marriage, my mother had not conceived. There came a day, while my parents were in the village on a visit, when she complained of a stabbing pain in her stomach. Her condition rapidly worsened. My father, far more shaken up than his wife, got ready to drive back to the city to see a doctor. Seeing his state of panic, his mother laughed.

'Your wife is now two bodies. Take her to lie down,' she ordered. 'I'll go into the bush and get her something to take.'

'What do you mean she's two bodies?' my father asked.

'She's pregnant.'

'How do you know?'

'I'm a woman.'

'But it's not possible.'

'Why not? Are you not a man? Were you not born with seedpods hanging between your thighs?'

'Mother!'

'And have you not been pleasuring your wife with your penis?'

'Mother, please!'

'Because if you haven't, then another man has done your job for you. Your wife is pregnant.'

'Well, in that case I definitely need to take her to see a doctor.' My father resumed his frenzied packing. His mother laughed at his agitation.

'Just do what I told you. Get your wife to rest. I'll fetch what she requires.'

'From the bush?'

'Yes.'

'My wife won't take any of your concoctions.'

She drew herself to her full height. 'Why not?'

'I don't trust that kind of medication.'

'I'm your mother. I took these same herbs when I was pregnant with you.'

'Times have changed. We have real medicine now.'

'Are you saying that roots and herbs which worked yesterday have forgotten their work today?'

'I can't argue with you when you talk like that, mother. But my wife won't drink any potion.'

'That's the talk of foolishness.' My grandmother had already turned away. As she walked off to the bush she shouted her last instructions over her shoulder.

'Get your wife to rest in bed as I told you. Set a fire and boil some water.'

My father obeyed her orders, and within an hour my mother's pains had been relieved by a dose of traditional herbal medicine.

As soon as I entered the house and smelled the mixture of sickness and quinine that hung in the air, I knew that no such remedies could avail today.

'Father!' I called out. There was no answer. 'Father, are you there?'

I turned to my grandmother. Her face was suddenly heavy and tired, as if she had slipped on a mask inscribed with the scars of time. She led me to another room. Here the smell was unbearable. On a low bed lay a man – or a horribly scrawny bag of flesh and bones that had once been a man.

'Father?' I whispered.

The figure wheezed.

I approached the bed and peered into his face. His sunken, immobile eyes seemed to take me in with no greater interest than he took in the void between him and the ceiling.

'Father,' I said in a quietly earnest voice.

He wheezed more roughly.

'Why? What is this?'

'Tra-ns-mu-ta-tion,' he brought out painfully.

91

I put my hands under him and lifted him in my arms, cradling him as one would an infant.

'I got a job. I wrote two letters to tell you . . .'

'He knows,' my grandmother told me. 'That's why he agreed to go on this journey. He wanted to see you on your way in life before leaving. This sickness had been skirting around him for so long, but he had wrestled with it.'

'Are you sure he understood about my job?'

'He smiled.'

'Does that mean he understood?'

'Look! He's talking to you.'

I looked. His lips moved, soundless.

'He can't talk,' I said to my grandmother, frustrated.

'You can't hear. He wants you to be like the wind. The wind travels wide and far; the wind has no enemies. And like the sun. The sun lives far away, but his warmth touches friends and foes alike.'

I turned to my father for corroboration. The faintest blink of his eye would have been enough, or the slightest movement of his lip. But his face was blank.

'Father,' I said.

A shudder ran through his body. Then he lay still.

My grandmother's voice became graver. 'The journey has taken the journey man,' she said in Igbo.

'He's transmuted,' I said.

I gently lay my father back down and went outside to suck in fresh air. I thought about the meaning of what had just happened. My grandmother and I present at the end of my father's life. Stunned witnesses. What must it mean to her, his mother, who was also present at the beginning of his life? How strange, I thought, that at the final moment I should speak so like my father. I was astonished, too, by the fact that, perhaps for the first time in my life, I had spoken English words whose meaning my grandmother had no problem grasping. A magic of communication, I mused, achieved at the mouth of the grave.

The world, too, seemed dead. The earth appeared unduly hard and dusty. A light breeze soughed through the leaves, which were yellow, like piss after a bout of malaria. A high odour hung in the air. The sun, also a pale yellow, was being swallowed by huge clumps of clouds, the firmament turning dull and grey.

I was racked by uncertainty. Had death truly entered everything or was it my loss that had coloured my eyes, disfiguring whatever they fell on? I walked back to the room where my father lay. His mother sat beside him murmuring a soft dirge about a fame borne on air, a courage that tamed tigers, a love so mighty it forsook the world, a spirit that traversed seven seas and seven wilds, demolishing demons in its way. For a while I listened to her voice weave words of tears, then I broke down and cried.

Chapter Ten

A week after my father's funeral, I told my grandmother that it was time to leave her and the village and return to my post at the *Daily Monitor*. She drew me aside and indicated a spot beside her. I sat down on the earthen floor and waited. She lifted her palms to the sun, whistling a melancholy tune. Then with her sun-warmed hands she began to trace the contours of my face.

'You asked me the other day how your spirit smelled,' she said. Her hands were still on my face. She touched now my nose, now my forehead. She felt my ears, then lightly drew her finger across my lips. 'Every breathing person has two smells. But the smell of your good spirit overpowers the bad. I'm not surprised that it should be so; you are the son of your father.'

Removing her hands from my face, she placed them softly on her lap. Then she fell into a thoughtful silence, staring into the open space before her. The awkward intensity of her blind gaze amazed me. She coughed, then fixed me with her calm, lifeless eyes.

'I told your father about your quarrel with the big man.'

'The minister?' I asked, animatedly.

'Yes. I told him about it. He was already very sick, but the news pleased him. I know you will ask me how I knew his heart was pleased. If I answer that I saw it in his smile, then you will ask me how my blind eyes saw a smile. And my answer is simple: I see what eyes do not.'

'How did you know about the fight with the minister?' I asked.

'Don't pester me with your questions. I was the one who asked you to come and warm your back beside me. Let my mouth unload itself.'

She paused again and began to rub her palms together, whistling. From time to time a relative or friend strolled into our compound to find out how we were doing. To their words of commiseration my grandmother would shrug and say, 'Death has done his will', or 'We can't fetch a stick and thrash Death for what it does', or 'Death is like a man who visits your house whenever he pleases. Even when you have barred the door.'

After the last consoler left, she cleared her throat.

'When Chukwu first created the world, Death was a man with two eyes. In those days he would call back to Chukwu's house only those men and women who had done their work in the world, people who had attained old age. But one day, Death came to call home a strong medicineman. The *dibia* was at that moment expecting delivery of a gourd of palmwine by the best tapper in the whole village. The old rogue begged Death to give him another day, but Death refused. He then asked Death to tarry and taste of the wine before doing his work. Again Death said no, that he had too much work for that day and that wine would only confuse his eyes. In anger, the medicineman cast a spell of blindness over Death. Since then, Death has taken away whoever he feels with his cold hand. That is why some children these days die before their parents.

'If Death were not blind, then your father would have been here speaking these words to you and I would be the one in the grave. But we cannot go and ask Death why he snatched away your father. Our people say that when a young man is not well girded and goes to enquire about what happened to his father, then what happened to his father will also claim him.

'Your father spoke to you before he went on his journey. You did not hear him. Do you know why? Because young men of today have lost the things of old. You no longer hear the language of things not said with words.

'Your father did not follow death like a lame man. He first wanted to know that you can stand in the world like a man. You must always remember that you come from a line of speakers. Your grandfather was the town crier for all of Amawbia. Your own father could have succeeded him, but he grew up in the age of the whiteman's rule. So he went to the whiteman's country and learned to become a new kind of voice, one that was heard far beyond Amawbia. Now you, a child of yesterday, have joined the line. You have begun to do what your father did and his father before him. What you scratch on paper can go and give a headache to a big man. You make powerful men stay awake at night.

'Don't fear any man, but fear lying. Remember this: a story that must be told never forgives silence. Speech is the mouth's debt to a story. You came from good loins. Your mother's breast was not sour when you drank from it. Let the things your mother and father taught you be your language in the world.'

With her hand, she again traced the contours and features of my face. As though pleased with what her fingers detected, she smiled.

'My own end is near,' she continued. 'My bones already warn me of death's approach. Yes, soon you will be left alone in the world. But you don't have to be lonely. The world teems with people. All you need is to wash your eyes. Learn to smell people's spirits. Run away from any man or woman whose spirit smells of evil. Find yourself a good wife, the kind your father married. True, your father didn't have a wealth of children. But look at you. Who can say you're not worth more than ten children? You must have a house full of children. Yes, have many sons and many daughters. As our people say, when sleep becomes sweet, we start snoring.'

She paused again, to whistle a tune. I thought of my girl-friends, past and present, but saw none of them as the mother of my children. I smiled, reining in a laugh.

'Laugh if my words tickle you,' she said. 'But remember what our elders teach: throw me away, but don't throw away my words. Son of my son, words are finished in my mouth.'

◆

The *Monitor* was in turmoil when I arrived back at my desk. Ashiki had suggested in his weekly column that the editorial board of the paper should be disbanded. The column exposed the board members as a bunch of overpaid and conceited mediocrities passing off pat formulas as considered opinions.

In public, the other members of the board affected a calm composure, but in furtive conclaves they plotted their revenge. They tried to persuade me to write a reply to Ashiki's piece, but I excused myself on the grounds of grief over my father's death.

The truth was that I shared Ashiki's sentiments. I had another reason, too, which was more pragmatic. My efforts to gain Ashiki's friendship had so far failed. It was not that he had rebuffed me; his attitude was more passive than that. He seemed to have no enthusiasm for friendship, as though suspicious of the complications of human attachments. Like the snail, he reached out warily, but mostly stayed in his shell. If I stood firm with him, perhaps he would one day relent and let me into that space he so zealously claimed for himself.

I had learned a little about Ashiki from others on the staff of the *Monitor*. The profile was sketchy yet fascinating, a jumble of facts and fables, exactness and exaggeration, certainty and conjecture.

In the late 1940s Ashiki had been a student at St Gregory's Grammar School in Langa. There he earned the nickname Monsoon by setting a record in the 100-yard dash that would not be broken for twenty-three years. He won a scholarship to Cambridge and after taking a degree in Economics returned to Madia to accept a position in the civil service. He became a notorious reveller, a skilled dancer of the twist, a man much desired by women. One night he got so drunk at a party that he broke the nose of a young man who had made a pass at his female companion. His victim was the scion of a wealthy Lebanese merchant. The aggrieved father put a price on Ashiki's head. Ashiki disguised himself as a Catholic priest to wait out the merchant's fury, but when it became apparent that the man was bent on avenging his son, Ashiki sneaked out to Ghana and then flew to Belgium. He ended up staying five years, enough time to earn two masters degrees and to marry (by his own account) a beautiful Belgian woman. After fathering two sons, he got bored with marriage and Brussels.

He returned to Madia on the heels of a huge consignment of stockfish he had ordered from Norway. In those days Madian merchants could make modest fortunes from the dry, nutrition-less fish. Ashiki moved into Langa Palace Hotel, a seedy but expensive establishment where rich men could enjoy unhindered liaisons with prostitutes, and began to run through his fortune. Evicted from the hotel after squandering all his money on women and wine, Ashiki began another life as a high-class vagrant, throwing himself on the hospitality of the country's rich and powerful. It was at a party given by one of his wealthy hosts that he met the publisher of the *Daily Monitor* and got himself hired as the paper's economics editor.

◆

A few months after my father's death, Ashiki and I would finally become friends, brought together by a shared experience of grief. I was mourning my grandmother, who had already been buried by the time I received a letter from the local headmaster, 'saddened to convey the tragic news of Nne's untimely transition'. Ashiki had suffered a far more shocking loss.

It was one of the hottest days of May 1965. I arrived at the *Daily Monitor* in low spirits, my energy sapped by the sweltering sun. Ashiki looked up as I walked in, and beckoned to me. As I approached he removed his glasses and ran his thumb and index finger over his closed eyes and down his nose.

'Do you remember my sister who was here recently with her two daughters?'

How could I forget? She was a lively and beautiful woman, returning to Madia for the first time since leaving for England seventeen years earlier. In England she had qualified as a dentist and had married and borne two daughters. These two girls she had brought with her to the offices of the *Monitor*, and the normally unsociable Ashiki had come out of his shell, showing off his sister and two nieces to everybody he ran into, boasting about their beauty and brilliance, jokingly warning me not to stare at the girls because they would marry *oyibo*, white men, not a bush African.

'Of course I remember her.'

'She's dead,' Ashiki said in a matter-of-fact voice. I had not

100

quite absorbed the news when he asked again, 'You remember her older daughter, the one you fancied for your wife?'

A redundant question; he knew that I remembered.

'She's dead, too.' The information came in the same anaesthetised tone.

I was confounded. How could this be true?

'A car accident?' I asked at last.

'No,' he said. 'Her husband.'

The man had hacked his wife to death. Their older daughter had tried to come to her mother's aid and he had turned on her, leaving her, too, a heap of flesh and blood.

Ashiki would say no more. He reached down beside his desk and brought up a bottle of beer. His Adam's apple working greedily in his throat, he gulped down its contents. I now noticed that four empty beer bottles already lay on the floor.

My father's death and my grandmother's more recent passing gave me some insight into what must be Ashiki's hideous pain. A thing like this, I thought with anguish, could destroy a man.

Ashiki set the drained beer bottle down on his desk. Our eyes met and he rose from his seat.

'Do you want to get a drink at Mama Joe's Bar?'

'Yes.'

There were three customers in the bar's common room when we entered: a man who drank in solitude, slowly running his palm over a bottle of beer, muttering to himself, and a couple seated in a shadowy corner, the bantam man telling his female companion about a street fight in Fernando Po in which he bloodied three men and sent one of them to the hospital. We exchanged pleasantries with Mama Joe, then passed into the bar's inner room, called the Executive Chamber. It was every bit as rusty as the outer room, but the customers who drank there paid an extra ten per cent – for their vanity.

101

Ashiki ordered another Heineken, I a large Guinness stout. At first we drank in a strained silence, for tragedy can tie the tongue. Then I found the courage to ask, 'This husband of your sister's, was he crazy?'

'No!' Ashiki said, and began to fill in the gaps in the story.

His sister's husband had lived in England for nineteen years, a beneficiary of one of those scholarships that were once available to Madians just for the asking. He had wanted to train as a chartered accountant, but had continually failed the exams. The man had not visited home since he left for England; he did not want to feel like a dullard in the eyes of his relatives, who would be apt to ask questions about his career. When his wife wanted to take their two daughters to Madia on a short vacation, the man had opposed the idea. They travelled anyway, but upon their return to England, the relationship between the man and his wife went from testy to turbulent – then all the way to tragic one short-tempered night.

A scowl came over Ashiki's face. 'My own sister,' he cried. 'Killed like a fowl! Who gave birth to this monkey that shat in the church!' He doubled over and sobbed inconsolably.

We ordered another round of drinks, and then another. After we had finished drinking I told Mama Joe that the bill was mine.

Outside the bar, Ashiki asked me to go on with him to a night club. His sorrow was so raw, his need to escape from himself and his thoughts so desperate, that I could not refuse. He flagged down a taxi and asked the driver to take us to Itire.

Chapter Eleven

There were only a few patrons when we arrived at the Good Life Nite Club and Bar. It was a ramshackle place with a small circular dance floor illuminated by blue and red lights. The air reeked of cigarettes and stale alcohol. The loud music made the furniture vibrate.

We found a place to sit at one of the tables in the drinking area. As we squeezed our way between the other tables one or two customers saluted Ashiki, whose exuberance made it clear the bar was his lair.

Two waiters hurried towards us when we took our seats, arguing for the right to serve us. Ashiki and I ignored their squabble. Presently Ashiki called out to a waitress, a tall bony woman. She beamed a coquettish smile as she approached.

'What will my husband and his friend drink today?'

'I'll divorce you if you've forgotten what I drink,' Ashiki warned her.

'No vex-o, my husband. But wetin your yellow friend go like?'

'I want you,' I said.

'*Otio!* My husband here is jealous-o,' she said, pointing to Ashiki.

'If I can't have you then I'll take a Sprite,' I said.

'Ah, but Sprite be drink for women-o. And children,' she retorted.

'He'll take a Guinness stout,' Ashiki told her.

'That is more better,' she said, ignoring my protest that I was already too intoxicated to drink more of the Irish brew.

We had just started our third round of drinks when two women drew out chairs and joined our table. One of them reeked of perfume too lavishly sprayed. They kissed Ashiki's forehead, then began to upbraid him for failing to turn up the day he promised to treat them to drinks.

'I was out of town on assignment,' he said languidly.

'Lie!' shouted one of the women. She was skinny and toothy and chewed gum in a coarse, showy way.

'It's true,' Ashiki insisted. 'I was in Port Harcourt for a seminar on tariff structures.'

'Tariff *wetin*?' asked the woman in pidgin.

'Structures. You may ask my colleague.'

'Your friend whom you have not introduced,' the other woman chastised Ashiki. She wore a light-green fichu.

Turning to me, she said, 'I'm Emilia. She is Violet.'

'Ogugua,' I said, nodding slightly. Emilia's hair, parted in the middle, made her seem at once comely and domestic. She looked faintly familiar, but my mind was too blurred. I wanted to acknowledge Violet, but her eyes were cold.

'Yes, Ashiki was away in Port Harcourt,' I confirmed.

Violet glanced sternly at me. 'You too be journalist, *abi*?' she asked.

'Yes.'

'Then you be liar.'

'Because I'm a journalist?'

'Yes. You journalists have sugar mouth but no truth inside.'

Emilia cast her a contemptuous look. 'You can't call the man a liar when you don't even know him.'

'Who says?' asked Violet in a raised voice.

'I say!' replied Emilia.

'Who born you?'

'You're crazy, Violet. That's your problem.'

'Who crazy? Na you be crazy! You and your mama and your papa be crazy!'

'Enough, girls!' Ashiki broke in. 'We want to drink in peace, please! Keep quiet. Or leave us alone.'

'You should talk to Emilia,' said Violet. 'She . . .'

'Shut up!' Ashiki snapped, frustrating her attempt to sneak in the last word. She rose and went to join two other men.

'I didn't mean to spoil your evening,' Emilia apologised to Ashiki and me.

'It's OK,' said Ashiki.

'It wasn't your fault,' I said.

'I'll understand if you want me to leave too.'

'No.' Ashiki placed a hand on her arm. 'I need to talk to you.'

When he told her the news of his sister and niece, she began to sob, asking questions through her tears. Ashiki's eyes too swelled with tears. He dropped his head in his cupped hands and began to shake.

'Take it easy, Ashiki,' I said, but he was already crying and fleeing in the direction of the men's toilet. I followed him. The stench of stale urine, sour vomit and unflushed waste overpowered his grief. He hurried back to the crowded bar, passed our table, and went out into the crisp air of the streets. He turned around and seemed surprised that I had followed him outside.

'I'm all right,' he said once we were out in the dark street. 'Go and keep Emilia company.'

'I don't think she'll die of loneliness.'

'I hope not. You know, she reminds me of my sister. Not so much in looks as in the way she speaks. Exactly the way my sister spoke. It makes it seem somehow incestuous, the lust I feel for her.'

'You've slept with Emilia?' I asked a little too excitedly.

'Almost. The first day I came here Emilia and I talked for a long, long time, over many drinks. I asked her to come home with me. Of course, I was planning to ravish her. But by the time she had got undressed I was already snoring. I woke up early in the morning and saw her still naked, sleeping beside me. Strangely, I didn't have a desire to make love. Instead, I felt the shame of a man waking up to the sight of his naked sister. I covered her body with a sheet. From that day on, I came to look upon her as my absent sister. Some days I would come here simply out of a need to see her – or to see my real sister through her.'

A brief silence fell between us, then Ashiki said, 'Take good care of Emilia. I'm going to take Violet home with me. I can't face the night alone.'

I returned to our table. Emilia sat composed, gazing at her glass of gin and tonic. She gave me a long smile. I took my seat and leaned towards her so that my arms touched hers. 'Ashiki has left,' I said.

'I know. With Violet. He told me.' She paused, then added, 'I hope she is good to him. Death is not a small thing.'

We sipped our drinks. After a moment I asked, 'Do you want to dance?'

'No. Let's sit and talk.'

'I don't have much to say,' I said. 'I don't know you that well.'

'All the more reason to talk. So we can know each other better.' She gave me a shimmering smile.

'I like your smile.' The compliment sounded awkward, gauche.

'What do you like about it?'

'It's the kind of smile you associate with temptresses in films. But yours is real.'

'How do you know?'

'I can tell.'

'Was Shakespeare wrong, then?'

106

'Shakespeare?' I had not expected Shakespeare to enter the talk.

'Didn't he write that there was no art to find the mind's construction on the face?'

'He did,' I said. 'But he obviously didn't have the privilege of meeting you. He might have known better had he seen your smile.'

'Oh, stop. You dangerous flatterer.'

For a moment we remained silent. Then I asked, 'Do you like Shakespeare?'

'I taught his plays.'

'You were a teacher?' I was embarrassed to hear the surprise in my voice.

She nodded. 'For almost four years. History, Geography and Literature.'

'Did you like teaching?

'I enjoyed teaching History the most. Literature was more demanding. Geography was a chore.'

'Why did you leave teaching?'

'It's a long story. And not a story you tell in a noisy bar.' She looked gently into my eyes. 'My flat is around the corner. If you come with me, I will make you some coffee.'

Her flat was a tasteful play of white and black. White walls, a black two-seater sofa made of fine leather, two white pouffes with Arabic patterns, a black dressing table on which stood an ornate Indian vase containing fresh hibiscus flowers. Around the vase, bottles of perfumes, powders, lipsticks, nail polishes were arranged in a way that suggested a desire for symmetry and order. On one wall, just above the table, hung a black-and-white photograph of herself, taken when she was much younger. The picture's background was delicately darkened, so that her smiling face seemed poised to break through the glass in the frame. Her kitchen, to the left as one entered the room, was meticulously clean, like a decorative unit, not a place where cooking was done. The covers on her bed were smooth, as though unslept in.

She made two cups of coffee and we sat on the sofa drinking and talking. I told her about my mother who had died when I was only four.

'Do you remember much about her?'

'Not alive, no. I remember her body draped in an immaculate white shroud, and my father telling me she was dressed like that because she was going on a special journey.'

'You must miss her a lot.'

'I was too young to realise I had lost her. But I have moments of extreme guilt.'

'Because you didn't mourn her?'

'No, because I caused her death. My parents wanted a child desperately, but my mother did not conceive for several years. Eventually, she became pregnant with me. By my father's account, I was so heavy my mother was certain she had twins in her womb. I was born five weeks early. By then her legs had become very swollen, her hips so painful she could not walk. She collapsed as soon as I was born, and stayed in bed with a fever for months. The drugs she was given didn't help much. She never quite recovered.'

'Who told you all this?' Emilia asked.

'My father.'

'He shouldn't have,' she said in disgust.

'He only wanted me to know how much my mother loved me. I had come at a high cost.'

We both fell silent. Relaxed now, and exhausted by my emotional time with Ashiki, I rested my head against the back of the sofa and yawned.

'You're welcome to spend the night here,' Emilia said, 'if you promise to be on good behaviour.'

'Where will I sleep?'

'In the bed.'

'And you?'

'In the bed, too. It can comfortably take two.'

'We'll both sleep in the same bed and you expect me to be on good behaviour?'

'Haven't you ever shared a bed with a woman without making trouble?'

'Actually, no.'

'There's always a first time.' Her expression was serious, but I retained a faint little hope.

'Excuse me while I change into my night things.'

She turned her back to me and pulled her blouse over her head. I glimpsed her breast, firm, its nipple black. My crotch bulged and I swallowed hard. She threw a see-through gown over her head, pulled off her skirt, then her white underwear. She casually turned towards me. I saw the dark triangle between her thighs, and a raw lusty craving rose inside me.

'Do you mind if I play some music?'

She pressed the play button on her cassette player. The rueful lyrics of a song in street pidgin filled the room. They spoke of the troubles of a woman caught in the trap of prostitution:

> Yellow sissy dey for corner-o
> Put 'im hand for jaw
> wetin de cause am-o?
> Na money palaver . . .

'Have you ever been in love?' I asked her.

She sighed, 'I will tell you my story some day.'

'Will you let me publish it?'

She said perhaps, on condition that her name was changed and no picture of her appeared.

We lay down on the bed and spent the rest of the night in talk and dozing.

When her clock showed 6:30 I announced it was time for me to leave. She went with me to the door. Smiling, she placed her hands on my cheeks, cupping my face. I shut my eyes a moment before her lips touched mine, opening my lips. The heat of her tongue made my knees buckle, but softly she drew away.

Just then I recalled where it was, several months before, that I had first seen her.

'Have you ever been to a party at Honourable Reuben Ata's home?'

'Quite often,' she said. 'I go there with Peter Stramulous. Why?'

'I think that's where I first saw you.'

Her eyes lit up. 'Weren't you the man Chief Amanka had a go at?'

I nodded. 'He would have been sorry if he had touched me,' I said. 'I was ready to thrash him.'

'It would have been quite a sight. Not to mention the scandal. "Reporter in do-or-die fight with minister".'

'Do for me, die for him,' I said with a laugh. Then, after a pause: 'You move in powerful circles, don't you? Tell me, where is this Stramulous from? Greece, Switzerland, Lebanon?'

'All or none of the above. I either don't know or I'm not saying. Take your pick.' She stroked my face. 'When next we meet, call me Iyese. That's my real name.'

'And Emilia?'

'That's for my customers. You're a friend.'

She kissed me again. Oh, my body boiled all over.

Chapter Twelve

Reuben Ata, at the time the country's minister for Social Issues, was the most flamboyant member of Prime Minister Askia Amin's cabinet. He was like those rare men in the world of cigarette advertising: ruggedly handsome, with a well-groomed moustache and sharp eyes. While the other ministers tended to be married, out of shape and dull, Ata was athletic, charismatic and – in his own words – an incurable bachelor. He was always quietly smoking a Cuban cigar, which lent him an added aura of sensuousness and power.

In terms of education, Ata stood somewhere in the middle of the cabinet: neither as educated as Dr Titus Bato, the brash minister for National Planning, or Professor Sogon Yaw, the former fire-breathing Marxist, nor as unlettered as Chief Julius Jupiter Jelowo, who held the portfolio of Traditional Matters. Ata had a number of dubious certificates from several London-based institutes: fellow of the Institute of Public Relations, chartered member of the Institute of Marketing, member of the Chartered Institute of Secretaries.

Four days after I returned from my father's funeral, I came to work and found a stylish envelope on my desk. I slit it open and read the strange message it contained:

PLEASE BEER WITH ME
ANY NIGHT OF YOUR CHOICE
FROM 8 P.M.
Reuben Ata, Honourable Minister for Social Issues

It gave the minister's home address. Why he had invited me, a journalist with a record of making trouble for his government, I could not tell; but I was curious and, in any case, in need of distraction from my bereavement. I decided to go that very evening.

◆

I arrived at the minister's home at 9:15 p.m. The gate was under siege by a crowd of women jostling to be let in. Three heavy-set men stood barring the way. These men, I quickly found out, were screeners. Now and then they pointed to one of the women and said, 'You, go in.' The lucky woman then squeezed through a crush of bodies to gain entrance. Once past the gate, she stopped to spruce up, then strode up the driveway with a gait calculated to mock the unchosen ones.

I waded through the press of bodies, fished out my invitation card and handed it to one of the screeners. He examined it closely, turning it over twice.

'I'm from the *Daily Monitor*,' I said, hoping that information would be helpful to my case.

'Ah! You're welcome, sir. Please go in.'

As soon as he uttered those words, I was seized by many hands as the women clamoured to be taken with me. It was only with the assistance of the screeners that I was able to extricate myself and pass through the gate. When I reached the house my heart was pounding. I paused outside the door to collect myself before going in.

The room I entered was large, high-ceilinged and brightly lit. A smell of food and cigar smoke filled the air. A band was playing blues, but nobody was dancing. People sat in small clusters, one or two men ringed by several women. Most of the

112

men were stout and middle-aged, all the women young and lithe.

A tall man came up to me – I recognised him at once as Reuben Ata – and extended his right hand. I shook it, and introduced myself.

'Welcome, my friend, welcome. I'm glad you could join us.'

'Thank you for inviting me.'

'The pleasure is all mine.'

He led me to a corner of the room where several cabinet ministers were seated, attended by a retinue of women. The women sat on the ministers' laps or massaged their necks. The ministers drank and conversed calmly, as if the women hanging about them were natural extensions of themselves. Professor Yaw and Chief Amanka sat together, the latter sprawled on a large round pouffe. Ata introduced me.

'You're the rat who wrote nonsense about me!' Amanka shouted, bolting up like a man stung by a bee. Ata put out a restraining hand.

'Rats don't write,' I riposted. 'Not even nonsense.' But Amanka did not hear me for all his raving and ranting. The other ministers murmured and grumbled that they did not want press boys at their parties.

'He's here as a friendly force,' Ata said, to appease Amanka and reassure the others. I wanted to shout a disclaimer, but my anger was too hot for words.

Yaw drew Amanka away. 'He's a young man,' Yaw said. 'He was obviously misled. We must forgive him.'

The ministers took up Yaw's words like a refrain. 'He was misled,' they echoed, grinning contentedly.

I shook with rage, but my tongue stayed cold. Ata held me by my shoulder and, gently prodding, said, 'Let me introduce you to other guests.'

Three European ambassadors cavorted with several young women who seemed engaged in a silent struggle to be the ambassadors' native sex for the night. The two African diplomats fared rather worse than their European counterparts in the attentions of women. Then there were a number of officers from the Army, Air Force and Navy; some European and American businessmen; several senators, and a sundry assortment of lawyers, doctors, architects and contractors.

Each guest acknowledged me with a smile, a nod or a handshake. Finally Ata took me to a corner of the room where a sturdy man with carefully crimped hair sat almost isolated from the rest of the party. His female companion leant against him, both of them enveloped in the halo of smoke the man blew from his cigar.

'Mr Stramulous,' Ata said in introduction. He then mentioned my name and affiliation. Without lifting his eyes, Stramulous nodded ever so slightly. His companion glanced up, fleetingly met my gaze, then laid her head back on Stramulous's chest.

My heart fluttered with excitement. Peter Stramulous was a shadowy figure in Madian public affairs, a man about whom people knew little. Nobody disputed that he was the trusted confidant of Prime Minister Amin; some claimed that he was the launderer of the prime minister's loot. He was known to be stupendously rich, a man who spent a fortune on rare sports cars, overseas villas, jewellery and horses, though the sources of his money were unknown.

'An impressive crowd,' I said to Ata at the end of my round of introductions.

'Movers and shakers, yes.'

'Every night, you have this kind of crowd?'

'Tonight is nothing. You should come when His Excellency is in attendance.'

'The prime minister?'

'Yes, he's here all the time. In fact he would have been here tonight but for some urgent national matter that came up. To lead a nation is no joke.'

'Very true.'

'And His Excellency doesn't joke with his work.'

'I'm sure.'

'But when he plays he plays hard, too.'

'Fair enough.'

'What do you wish to drink?'

'Orange juice, please.'

'What? Come on, be a man!'

'I need to calm down. I was mobbed at your gate.'

'Oh, those girls! Every girl in town wants to gatecrash my party.'

'It was frightening.'

'Believe me, it was nothing. Wait until midnight.'

'You mean it gets crazier?'

'That's the buzz hour. A girl even died.'

'No!'

'Yes! This is what – August, isn't it? Five months ago one lady died outside my gate.' The minister's face came alive with pride. 'Competition to get into Ata's party. This is the biggest party in town.'

'But to die for a party, that's going a bit too far.'

'The cabinet came to the same conclusion. We extensively debated the incident and decided that such a tragedy must not recur. That's why we took the prudent step of forming the Power Platoon.'

'A military unit?'

'Oh no!' he said, laughing. 'They are a number of girls – thirty in all – who are permanent guests at my party. We named them the Power Platoon.'

'Makes sense: you're in power and they're your foot soldiers. Sort of,' I suggested.

Ata laughed, then said, 'Now how about a swig of cognac? It's a highly recommended nerve-calmer.'

'I'm game.'

He pressed a bell. A man wearing black trousers, a white shirt, a bow tie and a black jacket appeared.

'Get a Hennessy for our honoured guest. VSOP.'

'Will do, sir.'

A few seconds later the servant handed Ata an unopened bottle of Hennessy. The minister passed it to me.

'Disvirgin it,' he said. 'It's all yours.'

'A full bottle of cognac for me? I'm not really much of a drinker, sir.'

'Hah! You're the first journalist I've met who frets before alcohol. As for me, I really like my cognac,' boasted the minster.

'I can see.'

'And I like cigars.'

'I guess they go well with cognac,' I said.

'Absolutely. And I love women.' He paused. 'Beautiful women, of course.'

'Uh huh. The three vices.'

'Or virtues, depending on who's speaking. His Excellency once said, in this very house, that with so many beautiful women in the world he can't understand why any man would ever want to commit suicide.'

'I had never thought about that.'

'Neither had I. His Excellency always comes up with original thoughts.'

'Yes, yes.' I paused. 'Umh, forgive me for changing the subject, but I thought to ask, what does your ministry do?'

'Oh, good question. The Ministry of Social Issues has a wide range of responsibilities. Part of my charge is to ensure the existence of social harmony in this country. You'd be surprised to learn how many disputes have been settled in this very house. I bring various segments of this country together. I also see to the welfare of my cabinet colleagues. It's not easy being a minister. You carry a lot on your shoulder. Members of the cabinet must have a way to cool off. That's why the cabinet gave me the mandate to throw parties. My colleagues come here to forget all the problems in their ministry. And to recharge their batteries. There's also a diplomatic dimension to the parties.' He moved closer to my ear and whispered, 'The ambassadors you see here will never send home a negative report about Madia. I make sure of that by giving them the most beautiful girls.'

'Sounds like a lot on your own shoulder, sir.'

'Yeah, but I enjoy my work.'

I nodded.

He said, 'As the air of this party I must circulate more. I'll find one or two girls to keep you company and help cut down your cognac. Don't hesitate to draw my attention if you need anything. *Anything*. Enjoy yourself.'

He went and whispered to two unattached girls. Smiling, they came over to me. Both wore mini-skirts and high-heeled shoes that accentuated their shapely, strong legs.

'I'm Susie,' said one, with a leer.

'Lucie,' said the other. They sat down on either side of me and began to chatter away. They rolled their eyes and laughed too easily. Then the one named Susie put her head on my shoulder and nudged her breasts against my back. A dengue-like heat overcame me.

◆

Madia was in the stranglehold of the most vicious kleptocracy anywhere on our continent – a regime in which ministers and other public officials looted whatever was within their reach, and much that wasn't. In comparison with the thefts committed by many of these crooks, Ata's passion for cigars, cognac and women seemed relatively benign peccadilloes. Everybody who knew him agreed that he was not a thief. He liked a good time, and he indulged himself at the expense of the nation, that was all.

Ata telephoned me the day after the party to apologise for Amanka's conduct. I went to his parties again from time to time. Gradually, he and I became close friends. He asked me to call him Reuben, saying that the title Honourable Minister sounded too staid and silly. 'It's one of those anachronisms we ex-colonials love to borrow from the English,' he laughed. 'And yet, I could not name two honourable things most of us ministers do in the course of a day.'

◆

I was at my desk one afternoon writing an editorial when my phone rang. I picked up the receiver and muttered a weary hello.

'Hallo! It's Reuben.'

'Hi Reuben,' I said, mustering more warmth.

'You sound awful. Are you sick?'

'Only of writing.'

'What are you writing?'

'An editorial. On corruption.'

'Can it wait till tomorrow?'

'Why do you ask?'

'My father is in town. I called to invite you to dinner tonight. You two would get along quite well. After dinner, I will clear out of the way and let you and the old man exchange views on corruption. How does that sound?'

'You always make these irresistible proposals.'

118

'Let's say 6 p.m., if that's okay with you. We'll have one or two drinks before dinner.'

◆

Like his son, Pa Matthew Ileka Ata was tall and imposing. Despite his eighty-three years there were no physical signs of ageing, none of the sags and droops that point a life in the direction of a grave.

A slight stammerer, Pa Ata spoke with deliberate slowness, in a tone that was perhaps a carry-over from his days as a school headmaster. He had been dismissed from the post and had spent two years in jail for assaulting a white superintendent of schools, a man who loved nothing more than to put natives in their place.

Over dinner, the old man recounted the incident. He told of the callow young man's penchant for rebuking teachers in the presence of their pupils, and recalled how surprised the puppy was when Pa Ata punched him. 'Are you aware you have just assaulted a representative of His Majesty, the King?' the boy had cried. In response, Pa Ata tackled him to the ground and proceeded to pummel his imperial person with more punches. We laughed over the story, but the consequences for Pa Ata had been serious. He was arrested within an hour. For the next two years, in detention, he was not permitted to see his family.

Was it this experience that had soured him towards the English, accounting for his insistence that Britain was responsible for Madia's problems, past, present and future?

◆

After dinner we sat pouring ourselves tea from a pot. Pa Ata said, 'Reuben told me you're writing something on corruption.'

119

'Yes. And I hear you're an expert.'

He shook with laughter. 'Well, I hope he told you my expertise is in the theory, not the practice. But I once attended Reuben's party and shook hands with some of the most corrupt people in this country. It was like being in a den of thieves.'

'Father!' cried the minister in mock reproach. 'Your own son's house, a den of thieves?' Smiling, he rose from the table.

Pa Ata grinned. 'You didn't hear me suggest you're one of them. But you must also be mindful of the saying about the company one keeps.' He winked at me as Reuben left the room. Then he asked, seriously, 'Why do you think we have such pervasive corruption in our country?'

'I've often asked myself that. I wish I knew a simple answer.'

'But do you not sometimes think it might be in the nature of our people? That we are born with itchy fingers?' Pa Ata's gaze was penetrating, daring me to lie.

'In moments of great despair, yes I have thought it,' I confessed. 'You hear all these stories about ministers using public funds to buy cars for their mistresses. Or acquiring European castles for themselves. How can you not think it? You go to any village and you're shocked by the squalid life there. The dust roads. Hospitals that have neither drugs nor doctors. The polluted stream water the people drink. The lack of electricity. Then, as you're trying to come to grips with a reality that seems to belong in the Middle Ages, up comes a Rolls Royce carrying some minister to remind you that you're not in the sixteenth century after all but in the twentieth. Then you're faced with the pathetic irony of the villagers lining up to hail the nabob in the Royce – the very man who's plundered their country. When you see things like that, how can you help despairing?'

Pa Ata said, 'You have spoken quite well about what one's eyes see in this country – though it's even worse than you think, believe me. Do you know why I asked you the question?'

I waited in silence; the old man continued.

'I asked because some of the things I read in our newspapers enrage me. Some of your colleagues talk the foolish language of the whiteman. I actually read a columnist who argued that we are born thieves, there's nothing we can do about it. And I ask, this thieving, when did it become part of our blood? In the old days, before the whiteman came and stood our world on its head, no man who was given something to hold in trust for the community would dare steal from it to serve himself. But today what do we see? Exactly what you described. I say, let's look at it and ask ourselves what has changed. There are two major things, if you think hard about it. One has to do with what white administrators did in the colonies. They stole, that was their main work. They were officially licensed to pilfer our treasures in the name of their monarch. They taught our present leaders all the tactics of stealing. The only difference is that the whiteman stole for his country, our people steal for their pocket. That is one.'

I tried to interject with a question.

'Wait, let me finish,' he said. 'The other thing – which is more dangerous – is that whitemen came here and threw together all kinds of odds and ends and called it a nation. None of us was ever asked if we wanted to belong to this new nation, or on what condition. We were all simply herded together into this huge compost, then misnamed a nation. We slowly began to forget how our ancestors had husbanded their souls before the whiteman arrived.

'Today, we're a people out of touch with our ancestors, a people who belong neither to the sky nor to the earth. So let me complete your picture of what goes on in our villages. The man in the Rolls Royce flaunts his loot because he believes it is his legitimate spoils. He has not stolen from those he considers his people, but from strangers. The poor people singing his praises

121

don't believe that he has robbed or disinherited them. They admire him because he has made his way in the territory left to us by the whites and has won his fortune.'

'Isn't it a sign of weakness, after several years of independence, to continue to blame the whiteman for the mess we're in?' I protested.

'If somebody deserves blame, you should blame them for a thousand years if you so wish. But, yes, you have a point.' He paused, as though thinking what the point he had just conceded was. Then he continued.

'I shudder at the behaviour of our so-called leaders. It's hard to believe these were the same leaders who asked us to drop to the dirt and fight the whiteman. Peasants and workers alike answered the call. Then, when the whiteman left, what did these leaders do? They took the owner's corner in the pleasure cars abandoned by the whiteman. They ran into the mansions the British left behind and barricaded themselves there. Then they began to remind us that we were not one people, after all; that we are Hausa or Yoruba or Igbo or Ibibio or Kanuri or Nupe or Edo or Efik or Fufulde or Tiv. Like the British they discovered they could rule if they divided the ruled.

'We began to fight among ourselves. They laughed and began to eat and drink. At Reuben's party you see ministers from different ethnic groups. But you never hear them exchange one harsh word among themselves. Why? They are united by their bellies, that's all.

'Is that what we all fought for? So that a few of us can eat and have swollen bellies while the rest of us go to sleep with hunger ringing in our stomachs?' He looked at me, the skin beneath his eyes sagged with sadness.

'Can anything be done?' I asked.

He sighed. 'Yes. First, we must ask ourselves, what is the identity of this space called Madia? Why does our present bear no marks of our past? What is the meaning of our history? These questions can only lead us to one truth, namely that we live in a bastard nation. Then we must decide what to do with this illegitimate offspring. I know this will sound radical to you, but the first step is to turn it into a completely different nation. Not by means of violence but symbolically, through our constitution. We must be ready to say two things. One, that any section of this country is free to leave. Two, that other people not now within our nation can become part of us. That's the only way of making our nation a living organism, one that can grow and contract.'

'I'm afraid such a transformation would be impossible to achieve.'

'Oh no,' he replied calmly. 'It could be done. Reuben must invite you to dinner again before I leave. I'll make it all clear to you.' He looked at this watch. 'I must retire now. Reuben's party will soon start, and I'm in no mood to shake the hands of thieves tonight.'

Chapter Thirteen

Several evenings a week, I would leave work and head straight for Good Life. Amidst the din of music, the spectacle of possessed dancers, the spirals of cigarette smoke, the clatter of beer bottles, the sight of men and women raising wine- or spirit-filled glasses to their sad faces, Iyese and I snuggled inside the shell of our private desires and despairs. We drank and joked and rubbed thighs as well as sides and exchanged pecks, arousing each other's ancient hungers in a variety of subtle as well as brazen ways.

Some nights Iyese became tipsy and melancholy, and let slip some morsel of truth about her past. Occasionally she began to sob quietly. From time to time her demons seized her more violently and I took her outside into the cool air and held her in a strong embrace while she wet my shirt with the storm of her pain.

Whenever I got drunk and grew bold I slipped my hand under the table and sought out Iyese's thighs. She would let my hand wander for a while, then she would remove it from the warm place it had found, put it on the table and softly slap it, purring 'Bad boy, bad boy'. Depending on how drunk she felt I was, she would either invite me to sleep at her flat – 'But you must promise not to try any hanky panky' – or plead with me to take a taxi home.

◆

The editor of the *Daily Monitor* at the time was a fellow named Austine Pepe. He had begun his career at the *Star*, Madia's oldest newspaper, in the years preceding independence when most of the paper's senior editorial staff were British and he was a lone bright native. He had been much beholden to his Anglo-Saxon mentors at the paper. They in turn had looked upon his industriousness as proof of the smaller blessings of the colonial enterprise.

As independence approached, and it became necessary to train the native talent who would take over and run many institutions, Austine Pepe was sent to Fleet Street to learn the secrets of British newspapering. He spent nine months of studious apprenticeship in England. On his return he was appointed deputy to a Bob Owen, the *Star*'s last British editor. It fell to Owen to let Pepe into the finer tricks of the trade.

The English labour was not wasted. Pepe the editor held himself and all who worked for him uncompromisingly to British standards. At editorial meetings (often without much provocation) he would brandish a copy of Owen's parting testimonial, which stated that Pepe was 'as good an editor as any to be found in Britain'. After reading it aloud he would hold up the piece of paper and pronounce the moral: 'Bloody hell! We all know how difficult it is to impress the English. This letter attests to my qualification to edit the British *Times* or *Guardian* or *Telegraph*. So, when I talk, I know what I'm talking about, for God's sake!' Pepe's sharpest rebuke to a shoddy reporter was to thunder, 'Bloody hell! No *British* reporter would give this kind of copy to his editor!'

But Pepe was not stiff like the English, nor did he prefer tea to a good beer. Outside his job there was hardly anything British about him. He was a small man who seemed to jump when he walked, as if to stretch his body. He sported a goatee streaked with grey that made him look like a wise village troubadour.

126

In his easy moments, on the odd day when everything went well, when he was not on edge about deadlines or sloppy reports, he liked to tell ribald jokes, gently stroking his beard. I liked him.

At first when I approached him with the idea of publishing a profile of Iyese, he was dubious. The *Monitor* was not a bawdy tabloid, he said. But I told him that this prostitute moved in powerful circles. For proof, I said that she was Peter Stramulous's mistress. His eyes lit up, half in excitement, half in doubt. He thought about it for a moment, then said, 'Bloody hell! I'll assign you the feature. On speculation.' Meaning that he would decide whether to publish or not upon reviewing the report I turned in.

That evening I went to Iyese's flat. I wanted to give her the news, share a drink or two with her and, with any luck, get a good blood-warming kiss and cuddle. She was not at home so I went to the Good Life in search of her.

I saw her sharing a table with Power Steve, a burly wrestler with rippling muscles and a ruthless reputation, and two other muscle-bound men. From a darkened spot I watched them, painfully conscious of my own smallness. Was I to turn around and go home, accepting defeat? Or could I bravely walk up to the table, beguile the musclemen with my charms and run off with the prize? The first option was shameful, the second dangerous. In the end I decided to advance, but to do so cautiously, giving myself room to make a quick retreat if things began to go wrong.

Luck: I saw Violet, pressing past me to join a table of excited beer-guzzlers one of whom had called out to her. I touched her on the shoulder and she wheeled around.

'Wey Ashiki?' she asked, recognising me.

'He's caught up in a meeting,' I lied.

'Ah, that man. Na so so meeting him do.'

127

'Our work involves a lot of meetings.'

Her voice mellowed. 'I sorry for him sister wey come die. Ooh, na devil work. Proper devil work.'

I nodded my concurrence. 'Do you want to dance?' I hoped that Iyese would see us on the dance floor and perhaps approach me.

While we danced, Violet made lively conversation that I neither heard (for the volume of the music) nor cared for. My attention was fixed on the table where Iyese was carrying on with the musclemen. She laughed wildly and leaned against Power Steve. Then she rubbed the wrestler's shaved head. Her jocularity aroused a dark resentment within me. I couldn't help imagining her in a *ménage à trois* with the three men, and the thought drove me to bursting point. Violet and I had danced to four songs and Iyese had not done anything to acknowledge me, even though I was certain that she had seen us.

What did it mean? The previous night I had spent a long time with her, drinking, talking, doing little silly things. Did it mean nothing that she had trusted me enough to tell me what her real name was? Or that she let me stroke her thighs and hold her while she cried? Was I, after everything, just another man to her?

Anger turned my legs to lead. When the fifth song began I thanked Violet for dancing with me, but told her I needed to go outside for fresh air. She asked me to buy her a drink. I bought her a glass of cheap brandy, then waded through the crowd of tables and chairs and sweaty bodies, past the table where Iyese sat, towards the exit.

The cool air washed over me. I drew in a deep draught, hoping to soothe some of the pain that I was suffering. Somebody came up behind me. I turned around and faced – Power Steve!

128

'Emilia said you should wait for her.' His voice was oddly soft. Iyese floated out moments later, her dress shimmering in the darkness.

'You look like an angel,' I said, enclosing her in an embrace.

'*You* look like a traitor,' she replied, gently pushing me off. 'Bloody two-timer! Ashiki told you Violet is good in bed and now you want to taste for yourself.'

Relieved to see her jealous, I decided to press my advantage.

'How about you? I saw you with the wrestlers.'

'Huh. They are not my type. Besides, if I had anything going on with them, why would I send Power Steve with a message for you?'

'Perhaps you told him I was your cousin or something.'

'I don't lie like journalists!' she said, sharply.

I was tempted to say something to the effect that I didn't flirt with whoever bought me a beer, but restrained myself. Instead, I said, 'Now you sound like Violet.'

'If you dislike Violet that much, why did you dance with her for so long?'

'To attract your attention.'

'Couldn't you come to the table and talk to me?'

'With the wrestlers there? I'm not looking to be killed.'

'Coward! . . . Anyway, let's go and dance.'

'No.'

'No?'

'I don't want one of your wrestler boyfriends to break my legs.'

'Don't be silly!' She made to walk off in anger. I held her back.

I told her that my editor wanted to read her story. After agreeing on a date for the interview, she kissed me, her lips cold. We parted: she, back to the bar; I, to the solitude of my quarters.

That night, I dreamt of a much younger Iyese, a simulacrum of the black-and-white photograph I had seen in her flat, and it was raining, and she was out under the downpour, and she was crying, like the orphan in the fable, and I was recording the symphony of her sadness.

Chapter Fourteen

Each evening, when the sun goes west to rest and darkness falls, many people yield to the body's sweet summons to sleep. But for prostitutes sunset is the time of awakening and the call to work.

'Why are prostitutes drawn to the night?' It seemed an obvious first question.

Iyese had taken time off work that night in order to tell me her story. We were seated on the carpeted floor of her flat, each with a tumbler filled with Guinness stout. Iyese had also bought herself a packet of Jay Menthol, touted in newspaper advertisements as a cigarette made with 'the modern woman' in mind. She lit one and drew strongly, considering her answer. My tape recorder whirred lazily, capturing the silence. A mosquito laced my ear. As I searched for it Iyese began to speak.

'Because the night gives us cover from prying eyes. Besides, our customers seem more comfortable at night. We are more shadowy then. They don't have to see us clearly. They can think of us as creatures of pleasure, creatures of the night, belonging to a different category from other women. They can't handle seeing us any other way. They're scared to see that we're the same as their wives, their daughters, their sisters. If they saw that their manhoods would shrivel up. That's why they prefer to meet us at night, in dark rooms.'

'A moment ago, you said prostitutes don't wish to be seen, either.'

'Yes, because we would always be seen with the eyes of prejudice, as the lowest of the low.'

'But as shadows, don't you always come out the loser?'

'Loser? No. Have you never wondered why prostitutes use false names?'

'I was getting to that. Why?'

She laughed. 'It's a sort of revenge. If men pretend we're mere shadows, then there's no use giving them our real names. It's our way of saying that the whole situation is false – that they, too, are unreal. It also signals to them that they are unworthy of trust. We don't let them know our real names, and when we have sex with them we don't let them touch our real bodies. A prostitute carries two spirits within her. With one she goes out into the night. With the other she lives a normal life. A false name keeps our two spirits apart. If we didn't keep them separate, we might go mad.'

'Explain it to me.'

'Take me, for instance. My real name is Iyese. The name connects me to the spot where I was born, to my mother's womb, my father's blood, my brothers and sisters, my childhood memories. It's the name with which I get angry or feel happy. With it I smile my true smiles, laugh my deep laughter, shed my real tears. It's the name with which I sigh at life. When I stand before the mirror, it's Iyese I see. When I dream it's the name with which my mother's voice calls across the valley warning me to run from the demons. It's the name that flows into my ears as water flows upon its bed of washed stones and white sand. Iyese is the name with which I see the world in the day. It's the name that reminds me of what contains shame or honour. It's the name with which I make love, when I do.'

She paused briefly, then continued. 'As for Emilia, it's like a label on a loaf of bread, or the name a vain man gives to his mansion, calling it Paradise or Harmony. Emilia is the name with which I return all the fake smiles that greet me at night. It's the name with which I utter whispers into men's ears. It's the name I use for my made-up moans and my faked orgasms. It's the name with which I throw my thighs apart for a stranger's erection and afterwards take his money. All my bruises and soreness I take as Emilia. It's a name that takes the rapes of my body so that Iyese may go unhurt. It's a name with which I am connected to the night and nothing else.'

'The false name acts as a shield against your night-time encounters?'

'Yes. I couldn't sleep with a customer who knew my real name. I would be totally frigid.'

'Why?'

'Because Iyese is not a prostitute. Emilia is.'

'Do all prostitutes experience this split phenomenon? This idea of being two persons in one?'

'Most, I'd say. There are prostitutes who can't imagine themselves as anything else. But those are the exception.'

I asked: 'How do people become prostitutes?'

'By asking to be paid for sex.' A bitter smile passed across her face, scarcely masking the pain that lay close to the surface.

'How did you become a prostitute?'

She stubbed out her cigarette and swallowed what was left of her Guinness. Her eyes, vulnerable and luminous, reminded me of the moon's magic when beheld by a child's eyes.

When she spoke, her voice quavered. 'Please turn off the recorder. I want to cry.'

There are tears whose flow ought not to be interrupted – such were Iyese's then. She buried her head in my chest, wetting my shirt, whimpering. It was some minutes before she grew still.

'You asked how I became a prostitute. It's a long story, but I will try to tell you.'

She drew her legs up and rested her chin on her knees. 'It

133

began twelve years ago when I was a second-year student at Madia Teachers' College.'

Iyese and her best friend had travelled to a distant village to visit her friend's uncle, a doctor who had trained in Russia and Yugoslavia and had imbibed as much Marxist ideology as medical training. This strange doctor, Maximus Jaja, at forty still a bachelor, had actively sought a position in a poor settlement that was cut off from the rest of the world. The Ministry of Health posted him to Utonki, a quaint riverine village of several hundred fishermen and peasants. To reach the village one travelled by bicycle for ten miles on craggy footpaths, then spent an hour in a small boat that plodded along a mud-coloured, fish-rich river. The life of Utonki revolved around that river and the fish that teemed in it.

Dr Jaja lived near the banks of the river, in a hut that smelled of earth. Iyese remembered listening at night, half afraid, to the river's raging voice as it travelled down to meet the big sea.

'What took your friend and you to Utonki?' I asked.

'Money,' she said, laughing. 'My friend needed some money for a project. She wanted to get some of her uncle's monthly salary before it vanished.'

Dr Jaja gave away most of his salary to the villagers. He had no use for money, he told them. The grateful villagers made up adoring praise-names for him. He was the magician who came by water. Son of the sun. Sun that sweeps the earth. Wealth that has found its way home. They repaid his generosity by adopting him as the ward of the whole community. He ate at different households while making his daily rounds of the village, a routine that started at 5:30 every morning and ended only when there were no more patients to be succoured.

Iyese had accompanied the doctor's niece to Utonki out of

curiosity. She had heard many stories about the man and she craved to see him in his strange world, in flesh and blood.

'Something magical happened the moment Dr Jaja saw me,' Iyese said, smiling distantly, as if the memory filled her with a sweet sadness. The doctor, who had never known carnal love, discovered it in Iyese, and expressed it with touching clumsiness. Iyese was thrilled by his attentions. She was twenty-one years younger than the doctor, but she agreed to take his hand and guide him through the caverns of love.

Dr Jaja proposed to Iyese at the moment of his first orgasm, and in the afterglow of their love-making she acceded. Later she experienced vague doubts and fears, but she was swept along on the now powerful current of Dr Jaja's desire.

Like many who first savour a delirious experience late in life, Dr Jaja developed an insatiable appetite. During the next two nights they traversed the village and made love wherever he chose. They did it twice on the banks of the river amidst the choral croaks of toads, the chirr of crickets, the chirp of birds, the drone of mosquitoes and the *plop! plop!* of fish drawn to the bank because the fishermen had withdrawn to their homes to sleep. Once, as they were relieving their passion in the shrine of the sun deity, Iyese saw the sacred python slither in. The python's eyes glowed on a small head, its richly decorated body radiant in the moonlight. It moved noiselessly, but its entry chilled the moment for Iyese, freezing all her sensations. Dr Jaja alone exploded in eerie spurts and songs.

On the first night Iyese had been worried that her lover's ecstatic cries might scandalise the villagers, but the next day she met the village chief, an old hunched man with a mischievous twinkle in his eye. Smirking, he asked her, 'Daughter, are you the one making our son a man?'

Embarrassed, she asked, 'What do you mean, elder?'

'Every child cries when it is born,' explained the chief. 'It cries to announce its arrival. It also cries because of all the evil it sees in the world. But every child has another cry waiting in the future, the cry of love. It is the cry that makes a boy a man, a girl a woman. Last night, we heard our son crying the cry of manhood. It put much happiness in our breasts.'

'Does nobody sleep in this village?' she asked in playful reproach.

'Yes, we sleep,' replied the elder. 'But a wise man sleeps with his eyes and keeps his ears awake. Your neighbour might call out for your help at night. There might be a snake snatching your hen. It is the ear's duty to hear these commotions and to rouse a sleeper. The cry of love delights the ear. May the sun bless you for showing his son the mystery of manhood.'

Two days later Iyese went back to college carrying in her handbag a letter the doctor asked her not to read until she was safely in her room.

'You may read the letter,' Iyese said to me, extracting it from a box-file that was hidden under her bed. 'In fact, keep it. It disturbs my nights when I remember it.'

The words sprawled across two pages in a cursive hand that was more like an artist's than a doctor's. The language sometimes read like a neophyte poet's:

> Some people are doomed with eyes that see little. I was one such. Some have hearts that know love only by giving, never by receiving. I was also one such. There is knowledge and there is wisdom. Wisdom is to know that eyes are good but seeing is better; that a giving heart is good but the heart that knows how to receive is beautiful and blessed.
>
> How strange that it took somebody as young as you to lead me to these lights. The village chief said you made me

a man. How I wish he knew how deeply. Now, I want to be the small seed which dies and decays in the bowels of the earth; dies and decays in order to be resurrected with startling, vibrant, magnificent life.

I wish I had known before now that the magic of the world often flows from the things we account too peripheral. If only I had listened more closely to the wise words of our elders who in their wisdom said, 'What one is looking for in Sokoto town is in the sokoto gown.'

A prodigal, I thought the truth lay in what the ancestors of Europe had to say. I searched for the matrix of Marx, embraced the delusions of Descarte, the cant of Kant. I was drawn to Hegel's heresies, to the fraudulencies of Freud. I dismissed my own patrimony as naive, atavistic and inconsequential. I imagined that all true wisdom existed in the tomes of Europe. I read them voraciously. Through them, I found eyes, but the key to seeing still eluded me. Yes, I harvested knowledge from Europe's soil but I found little wisdom in it.

I returned from Europe with a grand agenda for our country. But who was going to lend me a hand? Our finest talent, I found, had been consumed by cynicism, the youth had surrendered to despair. I, too, quickly shed the illusion that the world was waiting to be saved – by me and a small band of messiahs. But I truly wanted to serve, and if I could not serve my country I was quite content to seize a small corner and give service. I could live with a small dream; dreamlessness, on the other hand, would kill me.

So I asked to be posted to a small needy community. I asked with love, but the officer who sent me to Utonki did so with a punitive heart. For four years I have spent my revolutionary fevers in this small world. In those four years I have learned that the quality of service is hardly flawed.

Now you have come and opened my eyes to another wisdom: that service is flawed – can only be flawed – when one refuses to be served in return. You could not have come at a better time.

The same blubbery bastard at headquarters who posted me here has of late dreamed up a new way to crush my spirits. He now wants to post me out of here to – a city, of all places! He has written a memo to set off the process. In it he alleged that I have virtually been on holiday here; that no superior officer supervises what I do (or don't do); that I spread dangerous propaganda among the people, thereby flouting civil service rules (the specific sections and subsections of which he diligently listed). But the most unbearable part of his memo was his argument (and here I must quote him) that, 'The rationale for maintaining qualified medical personnel in Utonki does not exist in actuality. The people are accustomed to, and prefer, traditional forms of therapy, viz divination, herbal pharmacology, spirit medium, and other pagan rites. Consequently there are no tenable considerations to support retaining Dr Jaja in his present post.'

Based on this outrageous memo the Ministry sent one of its officers here to evaluate the situation. A mouth-foaming idiot! The first question he asked me was what did I gain from living in such darkness? A grown man like me, he remarked in astonishment. He said there were 'progressive' doctors in cities making good money and building beautiful houses and buying nice, nice cars. It was apparent from his accent that he felt that I had somehow interrupted his rapturous life in the city. When he found out that the salary they routed to me every month was shared with the villagers, he asked, the greedy glutton, could I let him keep some? When I said no, he tried blackmail. Was I aware that it was unethical to relate too socially with my patients? He could recommend that I be disciplined, did I know that?

I laughed in his face. A hard, derisive laugh, in his startled face. Then I told him that he and I spoke two different languages, that no magic of translation could ever bridge the gulf of mutual incomprehension between us.

He left Utonki, I am sure, with the echo of that laugh ringing in his ears. I know that he is going to be dangerous once he has ascended the throne in the miniature kingdom of his office. I can almost picture him in the chagrined thrill of meagre power, his quivering hand penning the verdict: 'After a thorough and exhaustive consideration of all the extant facts pertaining to the above subject, bla bla bla, I have come to the conclusion that Dr Jaja's posting in Utonki is not consistent with the Ministry's objective of optimising healthcare delivery. Bla bla bla.'

What options am I left with in this unfair situation? To ignore my redeployment and stay back? It's the option that most appeals to my idealism. But stay back and do what? The ministry would quickly withdraw all medicines and other supplies. Idealism – even I must concede – cannot synthesise drugs. Rather unfortunate; but without drugs a doctor becomes a mere bogeyman. I cannot operate in a situation where all I can offer my patients is the arbitrariness of miracles. I am left, then, with a choice that sounds to me like a betrayal. But, as I think about it, the betrayal is not mine but that of small men who would rather be gods!

As I brace to depart from these people, I am filled with

great hope – that the inner energy and natural cunning of all who dwell among forests are going to keep them one step ahead of their worst troubles.

As for my own situation I can only say this: my going to the city will not optimise healthcare delivery. But it will bring us closer to each other. Not a bad punishment, if you ask me! I used to think of marriage as something peculiarly absurd which only fools inflicted on themselves. That changed when I asked and you said yes. Now I am filled with a great longing.

I will keep you apprised of the situation with the chaps at headquarters.

With my bottomless love,
Maximus

Dr Jaja was eventually posted to Bini, a city less than an hour from Iyese's college. Still, he cried as he climbed on to the old boat that was to take him away from Utonki. All the adults and children of the village stood on the bank to bid him farewell, in silent tears that came from a deep region of their hearts.

Chapter Fifteen

Three months later Dr Maximus Jaja, escorted by seven of his relatives, arrived in Iyese's village to see her family and formally express his intention to take her, with their approval, as his wife. The short ceremony was called 'knocking on the door'.

'Neither Maximus nor myself was allowed to say anything,' Iyese told me. The oldest man in Dr Jaja's party spoke for him. The only time Iyese was invited to join the circle where Dr Jaja's relatives and hers drank and bantered was when she and five other maidens were asked to line up so that her suitor could identify her as the one he had come to talk about. Since Iyese's father had been dead for a few years, his eldest brother spoke on behalf of her family. As the day wore on and the gathering began to drift into revelry this uncle of Iyese's cleared his throat and addressed the suitor's party.

'I thank our visitors who have come to us from a far place. The message you bring pleases us. Your son who wants our daughter seems to us a good fellow. A bad man only asks his relatives to escort him to a fight, but your son invited you to lead him to the house of the woman he desires as his wife. You who have come with him are also good people. The day may come when we know one another better and I can call you not visitors but friends. For today we must release you. Your home is far and you must set off before the sun goes home and darkness swallows your path. If you were already our in-laws we would ask you to stretch out your legs and be comfortable and when sleep troubled your eyes we would show you where to put down your heads. But we don't know you that well, yet; nor do you know us. That is why we say to you, we have heard your knock on our door. We will put our heads together and discuss what you have told us. Then, whether we like our daughter to live among you or not, we will send word to you. We will do our work quickly. For now, you must hasten home so that nightfall does not catch you on the road.'

Despite her uncle's genial tone, Iyese knew that her relatives were not in the least enthusiastic about Dr Jaja's suit.

'Tradition forbade my people from saying a straight no to a suitor who came to announce his intention. But the strained look on my grandmother's face and a coldness in my mother's eyes told me more than words could tell.'

◆

The following morning Iyese was still under the spell of sleep when a light hand touched her leg. Waking with a start, she saw her grandmother perched at the foot of the bed.

'My child,' her father's mother said. With sleepy eyes Iyese looked up at the old one. Her grandmother asked, 'You are the child of my womb, are you not?'

Warily, Iyese nodded.

The old one touched her belly. 'Yes, you are,' she said to Iyese. 'You belong to this womb.' She cast her head down and fell silent, like one who had lost her way around words. The pause was only for effect, to increase the impact of what she had come to say.

Iyese knew that the visit and the talk had to do with her suitor. Her grandmother had not come creeping into her room this early in the morning in order to exchange the fables of Tortoise and Hare. The relationship between her and her grandmother had been special ever since the day Iyese came into the world.

'I was told that as a baby,' Iyese said to me, 'I would sometimes cry for no apparent reason. Nobody and nothing would console me until I heard my grandmother's voice. Sometimes I would refuse to sleep until she picked me up and rocked me on her shoulder. Other times, I would not smile until I peered into her eyes – and then I would not stop smiling. My grandmother had been born a twin, but her twin sister had died. Our people said I was that twin sister come back to life. As I grew older, people marvelled at how closely I resembled my grandmother. They said I was the picture of how she looked in her youth, just as she was the image of how I would look in my old age.'

Iyese faced her grandmother in silence.

'The morning seems to have taken away your voice,' observed the old woman. 'So, let me tell you why I always remind you that you belong to my womb. It means I will never deceive you. One does not mislead one's own blood. No! The earth forbids it.'

Under the weight of her grandmother's eyes Iyese swelled with anger and silently vowed that this was the day when she would break the spell with which the old one ensnared her. But how could she? How, when the bond between them was not of this world, but something forged in the country of spirits?

'The prayer of every mother,' the old one continued, 'is for her daughter to have a husband. A good husband, not just any man with a penis dangling between his thighs. A good husband is the pride of a woman. He is a tree on which her family may lean to rest from the hardness of life, a tree in whose shade they may take refuge from the roasting sun or the weeping skies. Are your ears open to my words?'

Iyese nodded, seething.

'Good,' said the grandmother. 'I certainly don't wish to waste the water of my mouth. My daughter, keep your ears open and hear my words. My insides were filled with joy when you told me that you found the man you wished to make your husband. When you told me that the man is a healer, I even danced the dance of my youth, that's how happy I was. As an old woman with a broken body, I wanted a healer as my in-law. But our people say that to hear is not enough; to see is better. So I said, let me not dance too much and break my legs before I have seen the man who has taken my daughter's heart. Yesterday I saw him with my two eyes. I thank the One who lives in the sky for giving me two good eyes. My daughter, my eyes did not find satisfaction in what they saw.'

Iyese made to speak but the old one hushed her. 'Wait, my daughter, let me finish. My spirit tells me this is not the man for you. Your real husband is still in the hands of the future. You will meet him and you will know.'

In a calm voice that concealed her exasperation, Iyese asked, 'Great Mother, what if I know that Maximus is the one?'

'Knowledge comes in different shades. Remember the warning Mother Mouse gave to Baby Mouse about wandering too far afield. Did Baby Mouse listen? No! He knew his way around, he boasted. But one day Cat caught up with him and made a sumptuous meal of him. The ruin of the world is that children no longer listen to their parents. You read one or two books, then think you have fathomed the mysteries of life. A wise child listens to the voice of her parents. We see things that the eyes of youth cannot.'

'Great Mother,' Iyese said, but again her grandmother hushed her with a raised palm.

'I am the mother of your father. He listened with open ears when I talked. But you — you dispute what I say. Please explain one thing to me: this your wisdom, where did it come from?'

Iyese knew that the question was more for effect than in expectation of an answer.

Having established her right to speak without further interruptions, the old woman now spoke in a calm, even voice.

'My spirit does not accept this man. A healer like him should not walk about on foot like a palmwine tapper. No, he should ride in a car. But this man of yours shambles about on foot, the dust accompanying him as it does the village urchins on their way to the stream. Then he tried to cover his shame with lies only an idiot would believe – that in the country of the whiteman many healers go to work on bicycles or even ride *kia kia* buses. Did he think he was talking to fools? We have seen other healers who went to the whiteman's country. They come back with big cars. You heard your man say he prefers poverty to riches. Does a sane man say that kind of thing to his in-laws? How is he going to find food for your stomach? How will he make sure you don't appear naked in the gathering of women?

'My daughter, the world has changed. This is no longer the time when everyone got the yam and cocoyam they needed from their own farm. The world of today speaks the language of money. You know the burden your mother has carried since your father died and left her with three children to feed. You need a husband who will wipe your mother's brow and relieve her of some of her load.'

Her eyes fixed on Iyese, the old one said, 'There's another thing, child of my womb. Who cannot see that this man is too old for you? When a man is as old as he and unmarried, something is not right. His people need to take him to a medicine man.'

'Great Mother,' Iyese began, sitting up on the bed so that her eyes met her grandmother's. 'There is no way a sapling such as I can contradict your talk. Who am I but your little daughter who is still learning the way of speech? All my learning is not

145

up to the saliva you spit out in the morning. My wisdom is nothing but foolishness where you stand. Great Mother, I cannot quarrel with your words. I can only try to explain myself a little.

'It is true that Maximus has no car. But that will change. He will buy a car. A very big car, and you will be the first to ride in it. I also know he is much older than I. That was one of the things I noticed when I first met him. But the first thing I saw was his goodness. He is a man of love. His love shines like the sun.'

The matriarch smiled with satisfaction. 'My daughter, you have spoken like a child born from a good womb. But I want you to know that love is never enough for marriage. If you were making friendship with this man, then you might feed on love all day and all night. But marriage is different. One washes one's two eyes in water before journeying into marriage. I don't want you to run back to this compound tomorrow and say that what you saw in this man you no longer see. Or that you have eaten so much love that it now tastes bitter in your mouth. Do you understand my words?'

'Yes, Great Mother. Maximus and I will have a good marriage. I will never run away like an *ogbanje*. Maximus will change. Don't our people say that whenever one wakes up becomes one's morning? That tree you want him to be, that's what he will be.'

Later that day, when Iyese's family met to discuss what message to send back to her suitor, the matriarch stunned the others by speaking in Dr Jaja's favour.

'Iyese has explained herself to me. The man strums the music that moves her heart. Iyese is the one who will live in the same house with the man. Our people say that the person most close to someone smells the tang of his breath.'

The relatives were lost for words. The person they had chosen as their advocate had betrayed them, and not one of them, man or woman, could stand up and defy her. What they saw as unforgivable treachery Iyese and her grandmother saw as something altogether different: the triumph of love. For Iyese it was also something else: the fulfilment of a promise she had made in a moment of ecstasy.

After the meeting the old one drew Iyese aside for a last chat.

'My words are not many,' she said, taking Iyese's hand and walking towards the *udala* tree in the centre of the compound. 'Nobody now stands between you and this man. But I must whisper a small message to your ears. A wise woman can take any man and mould him into the husband she wants. You must mould this man to be a profit to you, to your children and to your family. I know you are a wise woman. I know it in my marrow.'

'Great Mother,' Iyese said, 'I understand your words.'

Two years later Iyese graduated from Madia Teachers' College. Shortly afterwards she and Dr Jaja were joined in marriage according to the rites of her people.

Unlike the doctor's first visit to Iyese's village, his arrival for the traditional wedding was a spectacle. He was preceded by a convoy of eight gleaming cars, their upholstery draped in white. He himself rode in a black sun-roofed Mercedes Benz that brought up the rear. When the convoy approached Iyese's village, Dr Jaja lifted himself through the car's roof. A broad smile adorned his face as he waved to the villagers who stood along the dusty road, awed by the magnificent cavalcade.

The feasting and splendour that attended the event had not been seen in Iyese's village before, and has not been repeated since. Droves of people streamed into the bride's compound to savour the gay atmosphere, to see the dance troupes Dr Jaja hired to provide entertainment, to eat and drink, and to gaze at the cars. At the end the oldest man in Iyese's village poured libations and invoked the ancestors. He asked them to bless the new couple with plenitude, to ensure that they did not want for yam or cocoyam, to favour them with riches, longevity and children. Especially children, he implored, for he knew of the ancient curse that lived in Iyese's compound.

◆

'Four years have passed since the end of our marriage,' Iyese said, shaking her head. 'But one unanswered question still nags at me. Why had he changed so easily? Was it all of his own accord, without prompting from me?'

Looking back she saw how enraptured she had been, too absorbed in events to be shocked by Dr Jaja's metamorphosis. Why did he throw away that part of him she had first seen in Utonki? Did it have to do with the bureaucrats who belittled the work he did among the villagers? Was his spirit broken by his colleagues who looked on him as a naive idealist? Or did the change come from something that lay hidden within him all along?

All Iyese could say for certain was that not long after his move to Bini Dr Jaja began to change. He began to cherish the material things Madians believed to be the spring of happiness: cars, colour television, refrigerators. 'Especially cars,' Iyese emphasised.

He frequented the Bini public library to borrow automobile magazines. Whenever he and Iyese shared an evening at home, he would steer their talk to cars, reeling off terms that meant nothing to her: combustion, horse power, hydraulic range, thermodynamism. He stopped asking how her teaching was going. When she tried to tell him anyway, he frowned or yawned.

One day Dr Jaja returned from work and flopped down on

their black leather sofa like a man wasted by fatigue. Iyese, who was always home first, walked up to him and kissed his brow. 'How was your day?' she asked.

'Tiring and exhausting.' He gave the same response, she told me, day after day.

A moment later he said to her, 'I've been thinking. Maybe we should go on holiday somewhere abroad. England, Europe. What do you think?'

'Fabulous,' she said, without much emotion. For she too had learned to play the middle-class game. Overseas vacations were part of the package for people in their station, along with cognac, fine chinaware, dinner parties, and the complete set of *Encyclopaedia Britannica* that adorned many middle-class shelves, never opened, gathering dust.

'You know,' and he winked at her, 'to work full-time on the p. project.'

'If the reason you want a vacation is to procreate, I'm not going,' she sourly said, walking away to the bedroom.

It was already three years since their wedding and Iyese had never become pregnant. Once she had broached the subject of adopting a child, but Dr Jaja had been cold to the idea.

'My relatives would think that I wasn't strong enough to sire children,' he said.

Iyese's childlessness bred an anxiety that suffocated something inside her. It did not help that her husband had taken to speaking about their love-making as the procreation project. She had been to see several doctors, but none could pinpoint the source of her apparent infertility. One doctor had recommended hormone supplements, to no avail. Another had put her on an eclectic regime of medication and stress-reduction therapy. That, too, had failed. The rest had simply thrown their hands up in despair.

Iyese's anxiety was caused less by the doctors' uncertainties than by her own knowledge of the curse that hung over her compound.

Once upon a distant time, the story went, her ancestors had given away a woman of the compound to some colourless strangers in exchange for whisky, tobacco and gunpowder. They knew that Ala, the earth goddess, frowned upon such a sacrilege, but they had proceeded all the same. As the woman was taken away she had rent the air with her sorrows and called down the curse of childlessness on one woman in every generation born in the compound.

Even before her marriage, Iyese often wondered, in dread, if she would be the childless one among her generation.

Now the remembrance of this curse gave her a desperate sense that something ominous – an indeterminate darkness – was hurtling towards her. For months she endured the most wretched misery of her life. Her health, too, suffered: her body burned with strong fevers and a hellish ache pounded in her head. Friends, even strangers, noticed her dulled eyes, but not Dr Jaja, who seemed to glow with a vitality she could not comprehend, much less share.

One day, convinced that she was dying, she decided to try to penetrate the mystery of his happiness.

'I notice that you carry on as if there were no clouds in your life,' she said to him one evening as he sat in a rocking chair pouring himself wine from a carafe.

'Do you believe in dreams?' he asked her.

'Only those with lots of flowers. My grandmother told me their meaning.'

'How about water?'

'I'm not sure, but I think water is a bad omen in dreams,' Iyese answered.

'Some months ago I dreamt the same dream over three nights.

There were minor variations here and there, but it was the same dream in all important respects. For three nights!'

'What happened the fourth night?' she asked.

'It was dreamless. But on the fifth day I knew the meaning of my dream. I was in the bathroom when the meaning came.'

She listened, quietly disgusted, as he described the dream.

He is out fishing. He has gone far out to the river's deepest parts which are ominously calm and quiet, unreached by the cacophony of birds and crickets and toads. These depths teem with the strangest variety of fish, but they are also the river's eating mouth, thick with the odour of death. Only fishermen initiated into the magic of the river can broach these parts and still find their way home.

He is alone, casting nets, catching nothing, cursing his luck. A multitude of fish slice through the river or break through the surface and leap clear through the air, but all of them elude him. Suddenly, with no warning, darkness falls, impenetrable. How is he to find his way?

Instinct becomes his eyes, fear, his hands. The fisherman's anxiety not to become food for the fish; the predator's prayer to be spared the fate of the preyed-upon. In that instant of blind withdrawal he discovers that his net has trapped a heavy thing. He drags his belated prize onto the canoe and paddles feverishly in the direction in which his instinct points him. He paddles until his hands become numb with pain, the darkness in his head denser than the night that envelops him, then he abandons the canoe to its course. All along he has the sensation that the fish trapped in his net is observing his dread with fierce eyes.

Soon the canoe drifts to an area of dazzling light. The brightness rocks him, and he is so afraid he cannot cry out. His catch is thrashing about in the bottom of the boat. He looks at it, then freezes at what he sees, the huge eyes, almost human,

151

down the length of the scaleless body. Murderous eyes, blood gurgling within them.

The canoe begins to sink, softly, surrounded now by thick algae and water weed. The monster-fish breaks loose, begins to swim menacingly around him, teeth bared. He knows there is no need to struggle, there is no escape.

The inevitable moment comes; the monster-fish lurches with its fang-like teeth. He closes his eyes, visualising the world in vivid crimson. Instead his falling body is caught by human hands, a woman's soft, rescuing hands. He begins to ascend slowly, like a bubble rising up through the water. The resurrection is in slow motion, as if time had found a new way to mock human misery. His body, mildewy, rises, yearns for a sunbath, rises. The hands resurrect him, delicate but determined, raising his body towards the sun and safety.

Only when he has reached firm land is he granted a sight of the woman who has saved him. Tall, beautiful, black, pink-lipped, she is smiling at him – his benefactor.

At this point the dream peters out and he wakes up, a man trapped in the half-way house between remembrance and forgetting, a struggle to remember that merely leads to frustration because this, like most dreams, is inchoate.

The meaning came on the fifth day. Lying in the bathroom, submerged in warm water, lathering his body, his mind at rest, he recognised the face of his rescuer. Nnenne, the daughter of the chief elder of Utonki. The village elder had once tried to talk him into marrying Nnenne, a nurse who lived in Bini.

Whenever Nnenne returned to the village she put on an air of shyness, a false front through which her lack of innocence was apparent to those who knew how to see such things. It was said that in the city she was by no means an angel, that she wore thigh-revealing skirts and high-heeled shoes and painted her eyelashes with mascara. Some said she went to parties wearing no bra, so that her supple breasts heaved wickedly when she danced, tempting even the impotent.

Nnenne had schemed to capture his affections, but in those days his mind was not on marriage. And yet the idea had sometimes tempted him, especially during the harmattan season when he woke up in the morning, alone and cold, curled up like a widower, his member swollen with desire.

◆

Dr Jaja's affair with Nnenne had gone on for ten months before he told Iyese. By then Nnenne was more than three months pregnant.

'I still love you,' he said midway through his confession. 'Believe me.'

Iyese remained silent. She knew that in his rehearsals of this scene he would have pictured her throwing a tantrum, would have planned how to control her outburst. Anger was easy enough to deal with. Silence was more difficult.

'Believe me,' he repeated, prodding for a reaction.

I blame myself for marrying scum like you.

'I didn't mean to hurt you. But I'm not getting any younger. And our childlessness has become difficult.'

May she bear you a monster!

'Then there was the dream I told you about. For a long time I couldn't concentrate on anything else. There had to be a meaning to it. Why else would this woman appear in my dream night after night?'

Ask your penis.

'After the dream I went to see her. Just out of curiosity. Also to ask her how the villagers were faring.'

153

Lame liar!

'She told me she'd dreamt about me, too. And her dream also had to do with the river.'

May you drown in muck.

'I can assure you that this won't affect our happiness.'

Speak for yourself!

'I told Nnenne that you come first. Always. She's no threat to you.'

May the evil wind blow you off.

'You have to talk to me. Silence is not the answer. It's unfair ... I mean, unnecessary. Yes, it's unnecessary. Try to express your feelings. Please.'

May the eyes with which you saw this woman be gouged out. May the legs that carried you to her collapse under your weight.

'Yes, even look me in the face and tell me you hate me.'

Why? You must roast in a slower fire!

He fell silent, rose from his seat and began to pace the room. It was only at this moment of mutual speechlessness that the pain began to seep into her, to enter her through all the feeling spots in her body. As it drilled towards the centre of her being, she felt the room begin to spin in circles, slowly at first but quickly gathering motion.

The air became dense, blue; his face, before her, appeared to expand and dissolve. The room swam; her head rang with echoes. An anguished groan, involuntary, broke her silence as she slid into unconsciousness.

◆

'Are you absolutely certain this is what you want to do, Mrs Jaja?'

'That is the second time you've asked that question,' Iyese said irritably.

'Forgive me,' said the lawyer, 'but divorce is a serious matter.'
'And I am not a child!'

'If you were, perhaps my job would be easier. Sometimes adults don't think things through. Some come riding the tide of some isolated domestic problem. "My husband is a smelly goat! I can't stand him one more minute!" Or, "My wife is a whore. She sleeps with every man who asks! I want to cut her loose. Now!" There is no domestic scandal I haven't heard in this office. None! Many have come just like you. Through this same door. Some even tell their shameful secrets to my secretary while waiting to see me. You won't believe the things I hear. There's this woman who came – two weeks ago as a matter of fact. Said her husband made love to her only once in two months – if she's lucky. He's too busy running after the young girls of the city. Then the last time he made love to her, he gave her gonorrhoea! Yes, she came through this door and told me the story. "Quick, quick," she said, "I want a divorce. Don't waste time," she pleaded, as if divorce were a meal you could run into a restaurant and order.

'Her husband is a very important man in society, head of a government department. When he barks orders, his subordinates jump out of their skin. That's how big he is. And his wife brings me this terrible story about him. Why? Because he gave her gonorrhoea and she thought she was through with him. I asked her the same question. I said, "Yes, this man has done something terrible, but are you sure you really want to leave him?" Yes, she said, her mind was made up. I asked her to return the next day to sign some papers.

'Do you know when I saw her again? Four days later at a reception at the Goethe Institute. And she was with this same gonorrhoea vendor of a husband! I called her aside and said, "Madam, you didn't keep your appointment." She looked at me as if I were a filthy pig and said I should not disrupt her matrimonial peace. Yes, that's what she said. Matrimonial peace! As if I woke up one morning, put on a jacket and went to her house to sell her the idea of divorce. "Okay," I said to her, "it's wonderful if you have changed your mind, but I did some work and you owe me money." You should have seen how she sneered at me before she shuffled across the room and took her husband's hand. Tell me, what should I have done? Should I have approached her husband and said, "Look, I did some work for your wife and she hasn't paid me."

'You do understand my dilemma, don't you? Every case I take costs me money. But far too many people change their minds along the way. Which is their right, don't get me wrong. In fact I like to see marriages succeed. But,' he looked intently in Iyese's eyes, 'I also like to get paid for work done.'

'Well, let's cut things short. I will pay half your fees in advance.'

Iyese took out her cheque book. 'What does it come to?' As she wrote, a strange sense of exhilaration rose up within her, attended by visions of freedom. It was mixed with a faint feeling of illicitness, as if she were about to taste a sweet, forbidden fruit.

Chapter Sixteen

Three short knocks rang sharply on Iyese's door. Startled, she gazed at the door with a mixture of irritation and anxiety.

She had just finished telling me how, after the sad end of her marriage, she had made an impulsive decision to leave Bini immediately – too many of her dreams were tied to the city, as were the cruellest of her sufferings – and head, not in the direction of her village, where her family would receive her with resentment or pity, but towards Langa, a city she had never visited before but to which she was drawn because of what she had heard – that it was a vast, strange human bazaar where shame had no odour because people lived anonymously, where some of the most beautiful people walking the streets were ghosts and some of the saddest were corpses waltzing to their graves.

Another round of knocks sounded. I picked up my tape recorder, then lifted myself off the floor and onto the sofa.

'Are you expecting anybody?'

Iyese hissed with disgust and started towards the door. Another burst of taps exploded before she reached it.

'Who is this?' she asked in a harsh accent.

'Major! Open the door!' cried a man in a raspy voice.

Iyese opened the door just enough to put her face through. 'Isa, why do you want to break my door?'

The man answered, 'You didn't open, so I knocked harder.'

'I have told you I don't like the way you knock on this door.'

He laughed. 'Is that why you won't invite me in? You still like the way my gun shoots, don't you? Let me in!'

Hissing, Iyese made to close the door. The man put his shoe into the opening, wedging open the door.

'Okay, I know why you're upset,' he said. 'You haven't seen me for a long time. I've been extremely busy. Now I'm back, and I brought Major Penis with me. Bigger and better, trust me. And he shoots faster, too!'

Unimpressed, Iyese said icily, 'Go back to your wife.'

'Ah, but she travelled to Kano this afternoon. She won't be back for two weeks. Think of that, Emilia. For two whole weeks, Major Penis will be yours – exclusively!'

'I'm not interested. Whether you call it major or minor penis, save it for your wife.'

'Oooh,' the man said in a soft purring tone. 'Why are you treating me like this? Have I not given you good money? Clothes – have I not bought you many clothes, Emilia? Any time my wife is out of town, I take you to stay in my house. Is that bad? Think – what have I not done for you?'

'You have not left my door alone. I'm no longer interested in warming your bed when your wife is out of town. My boyfriend doesn't want me to be *ashawo* any more. Bye bye.'

She tried once again to shut the door, but the man gave it a violent push. The door swung open, sending Iyese reeling backwards until she thudded against the wall. She stood shock-eyed, winded. A stodgy young man bolted in, trailing a scent of whisky. He charged at her, cursing. Then he saw me and stopped. Our eyes met and stayed locked for a moment. Eventually I looked away.

He must have interpreted this as a sign of capitulation on my part. He turned back on Iyese, raging in a way that made her tremble. I averted my eyes.

'I will kill you without consequence! I will show you that

you're nothing but a common filthy prostitute! Because I brought myself low to sleep with you, you open your dirty trap and tell me you're not interested. I will show you who is who in this city! You find the mouth to tell me about your boyfriend. Boyfriend, indeed! Has he bought you half, one quarter, of what I have given you?'

Pausing, he looked around the room until his eyes settled on the television set. 'Yes, this TV. Who bought it for you? Me!'

He ran at the set and gave it a kick that sent it flying onto the floor. In another movement, he closed in on Iyese. He put one hand around her neck and leaned into her, trapping her, his face thrust close to hers.

'Who are you to insult me? Talk before I slap lightning into your eyes! I said, who gave you the temerity to insult me?'

He raised his right hand swiftly. Iyese shut her eyes, wincing. I sprang forward and grabbed his hand just in time. He glowered at me as though taking my measure, weighing an appropriate response.

'It's enough,' I said, letting go of him. 'You have made your point.'

I half expected him to come at me, but thanks to the karate training I had had at university I was ready to disable him with a kick in the groin. He seemed to consider the option of fighting me, but instead he turned and fixed Iyese with a long hard glare, then wheeled around and walked away.

'Who is he?' I asked after he had gone.

'Isa Palat Bello. He's a major in the army.'

'You have known him for long?'

'I met him the first week I arrived in Langa. The woman I was staying with, a friend from high school, took me to a party at the Officers' Mess. He was there, hopelessly drunk. I found him charming. I agreed to go to his house. There, I saw pictures on the walls, of him, his wife and their four daughters. The shock hit me: I had accompanied a married man to his house! His wife and their children had travelled to the North to see his father, the emir of Gabira. I said I must leave immediately, but he began to plead. Yes, like a helpless baby. Naively, I agreed to spend the night, thinking, what can a drunk man do?

'He raped me twice that night. When I threatened to report his unfaithfulness to his wife he laughed and said his religion entitled him to four wives and any number of concubines. I became his standby; whenever his wife went away he called me to warm his bed. Then three months ago he told me he had three other daughters by two other women, but that he planned to marry any woman who gave him a son. I told him of my childlessness and he stopped coming around – until today.'

'You bore a grudge, then? You felt he deserted you?'

'Deserted? No! I was relieved. I had tried to break off our relationship once before.'

'And?'

She laughed. 'He slapped me until my eyes saw lightning. Then he raped me, laughing.'

'You should have reported him to the police.'

She sighed, exasperatedly. 'Don't you live in this country? The police told me that the law does not cover people like me.'

'What did they mean?'

'They asked if he was my husband. I said no. Was he my sugar daddy? I said I didn't know what that meant. So they asked, was he married? I said yes. And did he spend money on me? I answered yes, from time to time. Then the officer in charge said, "*Chikena*, he's your sugar daddy. He can beat you." I left the police station in tears.'

'And did he ever beat you again?'

'Many times. He once told me he likes it when a woman cries.'

'A sick man! Why did you stay with a man who treated you like filth?'

'I don't know the answer.'

'Was it the money? The things he bought for you?'

'After my marriage, material things sickened me. I wish he would set fire to this house and destroy everything he's ever bought me, even everything I own. Spare my life is all I ask, because I want to be happy again.' She looked at me with misty eyes.

'Where do monsters like him come from?' I asked aloud.

'A friend of his – he and Isa grew up together and joined the army the same day – once said to me that Isa has a good heart but a bad mouth. And that whisky causes him to go mad. It was also this man who told me about Isa's military training in England.'

◆

Isa Palat Bello's road to a career in the army began the day he went through his father's photo album and saw a picture that made an impression on his young mind. In it, Isa's father, resplendent in his emir's regalia, stood shoulder to shoulder with a white army officer. The whiteman cradled Isa, then a toddler, in his arms. The officer's name was Colonel Mark Brady, once the British commander of the Royal West African Frontier Force. The colonel's whiskers were long, his eyebrows thick, his eyes small but bright. Bello was charmed by Brady's looks, especially his uniform: creaseless and clean, it suggested masculine valour. Brady's erect posture in the photograph spoke of the Englishman's power: Isa had seen other photographs in which other whitemen, standing beside his father, drew down their heads or cast down their eyes.

The British officer had encouraged the emir to send his first son to England for military training. The emir was impressed by the colonel's talk about the powerful role the military stood to play in Madia's post-Independence history.

'Think what an advantage it would be to have kith and kin in the army, to look out for your interests,' the Britisher told the emir, between gulps of hot tea laced with White Horse whisky.

Isa was a willing recruit. As soon as he was old enough he journeyed to England and, along with five other African cadets from Madia, Ghana and Sierra Leone, began his training at the military academy in Sandhurst. It was there that he first held and fired a gun – and so began to understand the contraption's awful power and the source of Brady's confidence.

As a Moslem and the son of an emir Isa was supposed to abhor alcohol. But the unfriendly coldness of England had made him lonely, low-spirited and open to temptation. He began to drink, first in small quantities, relishing the wave of calmness that washed over him after a swig or two of whisky, then less moderately. The liquor did things to him, made him prone to mood swings and bouts of excess, of both niceness and nastiness.

In England the destructiveness of his unpredictable moods was limited. If he was in good spirits he shared the fellowship of the other trainees. When he became surly, he withdrew to his private quarters or visited a brothel and worked off his fury on some poor English prostitute.

By the time he returned from England he was a serious alcoholic. According to the friend who explained this to Iyese, he had also begun to exploit his mood swings to display his power to others. He had fallen in love with the idea of himself as a man from whom people skulked away in dread. Despite his father's entreaties, threats and the final extreme measure of

162

banishing him from the palace, he went on drinking. He would not change, even after he lost one eye in a fight.

◆

'You knew he would be furious to hear you mention a boyfriend.'

She nodded.

'So why take the risk?'

She glanced up at the ceiling, biting her lip. Then she looked at me and smiled. 'Being in love made me daring.'

'Who are you in love with?'

The answer was in her smile. With a sensation compounded of lust, longing, tenderness and vague fear, I went to her. Conjoined at last, we lost ourselves in the unity of desire. We floated on a spumy lake, weightless, two entranced bodies.

Throughout the night our minds discovered new hungers and our bodies, entwined again and again, sated them.

In the morning I fetched my tape recorder, ready to leave. Iyese lay in bed, naked and graceful. While I looked at her she slightly opened her eyes and stretched the sides of her mouth in a sleepy smile. 'When will I see you again?

'This evening,' I said. 'I'll come over after work.'

Chapter Seventeen

I did not return that evening.

At the day's editorial meeting, my eyes blinked uncontrollably as I struggled against sleep, exhausted by the repeated love-making of the previous night. Eventually I nodded off, waking only when my head dropped sharply sideways. Some time must have passed, for my colleagues were gathering their papers and rising from their seats. I picked up my own papers and left, wondering whether I had snored.

I barely stayed awake in the taxi that drove me home. I ran up the stairs to my second-floor flat, kicked off my shoes, and slumped into bed. As I geared into deep sleep my room seemed to rotate in a whirling motion.

A rumbling in my stomach woke me up. It was past midnight. Too hungry to sleep, but too tired to get up and prepare food, I lay in bed and thought about Iyese, which soon became a way of thinking about myself, and about my mother, my grandmother and my father. What would they have thought about my relationship with Iyese? Would they have seen her primarily as a prostitute, and our friendship as therefore profane? Or would they have been moved by her spirit, her struggle for a dignified existence in circumstances so dire and inhuman? Weighing these questions, I lost myself, once again, to sleep.

◆

The next day, on my way to work, I stopped to see Iyese. There was no response to my first knock. I knocked again, harder. Silence still answered me. I gripped the doorknob and turned it. Much to my surprise the door opened.

'Iyese,' I called out, walking in. Hearing no answer, I shifted the partition that led to her bedroom. The room reeked of sweat. She was in bed, naked, spread-eagled, a pillow lodged between her thighs.

'Ah, you're home,' I said, with relief.

She looked at me with tired eyes, silent.

'I hope you haven't been in bed ever since I left yesterday.'

Silence.

'I made a total fool of myself at the office. I slept through the editorial meeting. I went home after the meeting for a quick nap, planning to return here refreshed. You can imagine the rest of the story.'

Silence.

'You left your door open. Don't you think you should be more careful?'

Tears rolled off the side of her face. Speechless, I watched her cry. After a few minutes she wiped the tears with the back of her hand.

'He came back,' she said.

'Isa?' I said in dread.

'He came with three men. They had daggers.'

My blood ran cold. 'What happened?'

'The men pinned me to the bed. Then Isa stabbed my vagina with a dagger. I started bleeding. That's when he entered me with his penis.'

A sensation of horror swelled inside my head. 'Oh!' I cried.

'It was like the stab of the knife, but more painful.'

'Despicable cretins!'

She lifted the pillow from between her legs. I flinched from the sight of wet blood.

'When did this happen?'

'Yesterday, about six in the evening. I heard their knock and thought it was you. As soon as I opened the door one of them grabbed me and covered my mouth. They pushed me down on the bed and forced apart my legs. Isa brought out his dagger and said he wanted to teach my vagina a lesson.'

'What did you do?'

'What could I do? I refused to cry or beg. But I silently begged death to come and take me away.'

'No,' I said. 'It's those bloody beasts who deserve to die.'

'Good thing you didn't walk in. Isa said he and his men were going to cut off your penis.'

'Cowards! I wish I had run into them!'

'I have been bleeding since they left. This is the second pillow.'

She pointed to the floor beside her bed, where a pillow lay, dark-red with blood.

'You've lost too much blood. I must take you to a hospital.'

'No,' she said, sobbing. 'I'm ready to die today. This kind of life has no meaning.'

'Iyese, this is no time to be fatalistic. Let me help you to get dressed.'

I reached for her hand and tried to help her up onto her feet, but she fell back on the bed, crying, 'Let me die! Let me die today!'

In the commotion I did not hear the door open. I started when a female voice asked, 'Emilia, which kind madness be this?' Turning sharply, I saw Violet.

'For two days you never come to Good Life. Everybody dey ask me, "Your friend, Emilia, she well so?" So I say make I come find out. Wetin be your problem?'

Iyese kept up her wailing, calling on death to come immediately.

Violet fixed me with half-accusing eyes, seeking some explanation.

'They attacked her,' I said, not knowing what details to add.

'Who be they?' Violet asked.

'Four brutes.'

Iyese had now calmed down, sobbing quietly.

'Emilia, who attacked you?'

'Isa,' Iyese answered.

'Isa. That man again?'

'He came with three men. They beat me with a knife.' She lifted the blood-soiled pillow. Violet recoiled.

'Na blood be this?' she asked. Iyese's tear-drenched eyes confirmed her fears.

'Forbid bad thing!' exclaimed Violet.

'I tried to persuade her to see a doctor,' I said to Violet.

'Don't worry,' she said. 'That one be my work.' She turned to Iyese and began to give instructions. 'You must go to hospital quick quick. But first I must boil hot water to wash you. Then I go escort you to hospital.'

The water boiled in a short time. Violet soaked a hand towel in the hot water, squeezed off the water, then dabbed the bleeding wound while Iyese screamed. When the cleaning was done, Violet fetched a loose-fitting blouse from the closet and handed it to Iyese.

'*Oya*,' Violet ordered when Iyese was dressed. 'Get up and make we begin go.'

Iyese tried to stand but winced. She tried again, her eyes tightly shut, teeth gritted, but again crumpled in bed. Violet and I each took one of her arms and heaved her up. Supported, she stood, her legs drawn apart, as if a wedge were lodged between them.

'It burns,' she cried, trying to throw herself back on the bed.

Violet and I held on to her. She began to walk with us, each step preceded by an agonised contortion of her face and followed by a moment of rest, to rein in the pain, to gather the strength for the next one.

At last we got her out on to the street. A taxi drove up and stopped. Iyese grimaced as we helped her into the back seat.

I directed the driver to the hospital and thanked Violet for taking Iyese. I said to Iyese that I would see her soon. The taxi zoomed off. I stood at the spot to wait for another taxi to take me to my office.

♦

The sight and smell of Iyese's blood stayed with me as I rode to work. I felt as if I were choking. I wound down the car's window and shut my eyes, trying to conjure up other images. Gore infected every picture I saw in my mind's eye. In the end, unable to escape the memory of what I had seen, I let my mind return to what it dreaded, to the sight of the pillows drenched with Iyese's blood, her grimaces and groans, the despairing anguish in her voice when she told me what Isa and his thugs had done to her.

Beads of perspiration sprouted on my forehead. My teeth chattered. The driver, watching me through his rearview mirror, asked, 'Are you all right, sir?'

'Yes,' I said. 'Don't mind about me.'

But I was not at all sure that I really was all right. In spite of myself, I was beginning to see the situation in the light of my own interest and safety. My anger at Isa Palat Bello and his minions was becoming mixed with fear for myself, lest I, too, fall victim to their butchery. Slowly, the fear encircled the anger, nibbling away at it. In the end the outrage was in the belly of the fear, the anger was eclipsed.

Something told me that Iyese would count on me to avenge her. But how? With what tools could I stand up to her violators? A pen? Against men who had daggers? Moral indignation? Against men with guns?

Then I pictured my colleagues on the editorial board having a laugh at my expense. *Boy, you were asked to tell the story, not to taste it! The test of the story is in the doing! Exhaustive exploration of all the issues! Fellows, our friend found ways and means of probing. Now we know the meaning of in-depth reporting!*

'No!'

The word escaped my mouth of its own accord. The driver looked sharply in the mirror. 'No what, sir?'

'I'm sorry,' I said. 'I didn't mean to think aloud.'

Once at the office I headed to see the editor. He was on the phone when I entered. He ignored me, shouting into the mouthpiece as though to a deaf person. As I turned to leave, in no mood to wait, he rang off and turned to address me. 'Yes?'

'I'm not doing the prostitute's story,' I said tightly.

'Bloody nice to hear that. May I ask why you changed your mind?'

'The story is flat.'

'What do you mean flat? I recall you said there was some bloody important human angle there. To speak nothing of the prospect of getting tidbits on Stramulous. What has changed?'

'Well, I interviewed the woman. There's nothing to her story.'

He considered this, then shrugged. 'Bloody hell, if you say so. I was uncertain of the story from the beginning.'

I left his office with a heavy heart. My mouth felt gummy and sour as I pictured Iyese in her hospital bed, sewn up, still sore, her slightest movement accompanied by excruciating pain. I entered her head and glimpsed her dreams of a new life, her

170

hopes that darkness would yield to light, that the sun was certain to break through the clouds to warm her world.

Perhaps she imagined that I could be that sun. Perhaps I was her faith: *Nke iru ka*. The future is vaster and greater than the past. *Echi di ime*. The future is pregnant. Did she nurse the hope that I would help her to build a tranquil, happy life out of her ruins? That I would save her and help her to start over again?

Her dreams crushed me with their weight. Better to make her understand who I really was. That my fears outweighed her needs. That I would never take on a man with a gun. That, while I enjoyed the moments when our two bodies were fused, I was afraid of the scandal into which her name and history might drag me. That for the two of us there was no future, only a few feeble memories. That I was not her sun but something altogether damp and clammy. That the besotting power of her sex and all the shame that came with it had rendered me nerveless.

That, finally, I could not bear to see her again.

Chapter Eighteen

Night visions began to poach my peace. Unable to sleep or to rest, I would lie still in a dark made unfamiliar by demons, scared of what might bare its face if I turned on the light. Breathing hard, waiting for the figures in the dark to disappear, I would be tormented by the feeling that I had again entered Iyese's head. Against my will I eavesdropped on her thoughts and mapped her body's aches and pains. Was this my punishment for befriending and deserting her?

◆

A month after I last saw Iyese, her letter arrived, the first of several she would write as each month passed. In each letter she addressed me as 'Dear O'. I knew it was a play on the first letter of my name, but it still left me with a nagging uneasiness. Did she also mean 'O' as in nought? 'O' as cipher, zero – an allusion to my sudden absence from her life?

> It's been almost a month since I last saw you. I don't
> remember offending you in any way. If you've decided, for
> reasons of your own, not to see me again, that's fine. Not
> fine because I don't care about your friendship, but
> because I must respect your wishes, however sad they may
> make me.
> A lot has happened since I last saw you. Part of it is

good news, but I must wait to see what tomorrow will bring.

My regards to Ashiki. He, too, has not come to Good Life for some time. Violet said they had a big quarrel, but I didn't ask for the details.

Love,
Iyese, 12 June

This is the second month of your absence. I keep running into people who look just like you. Or sound like you. I went to Tejuosho market yesterday to shop for shoes. Among the crowd, I saw the head of a man I could have sworn was you. Dropping everything, I pushed my way through the crowd until, out of breath, I caught up with him. I tapped him on the shoulder, expecting to see your face when he turned around. Well, the man turned around, smiling, but he was a total stranger! And he was with his wife! I began to explain, but the woman's angry eyes reduced me first to stammering, then silence. She dragged her husband off, as if he was in danger of being abducted.

Is this madness or delusion? Or is it love that makes me see you everywhere? Surely, you're thinking of me, too?

Even if I'm going mad, I don't care. Love is growing inside me.

Take care.
Love, Iyese, 13 July

Sometimes I cry thinking about you, but most often I smile.

Isa came by two days ago. He said he wanted to apologise for what he did. He brought money and clothes, but I refused to take anything from him. He left everything on my couch when he left. I threw the clothes out and gave the money to beggars at Oshodi bus stop. He said he is going away in a few months for a course in Pakistan. Something to do with logistics – I wasn't listening attentively. He plans to stop over in Paris and Amsterdam on his way back and asked me what I would like him to bring me. I didn't answer him, so he said he knows what I like. All I want is to be left alone. Sometimes in my sleep I see him and the three men who held me down the day he hurt me. Only death will make me forget the pain.

Do I burden you with my sad memories? I am actually quite happy, even though I miss you.

Iyese, 8 August

Today is the fourth month since the day you put me in a taxi and then disappeared. Is this absence forever?

I love you.

Iyese, 10 September

One afternoon I was absorbed in some research in the *Monitor*'s library when, out of the corner of my eye, I saw someone standing behind me. I wheeled around.

'Ashiki!' I exclaimed. 'How long have you been there?'

'Long enough to have been dangerous, if I were an enemy.'

'Have you come to read?'

'Not really. I was asking around for you and somebody said you were seen heading in this direction. I have a letter for you. A very important letter, if I may say so.'

'Important letter? For me?'

Taking the envelope from him, I recognised Iyese's hand-writing. 'Oh,' I said, half in relief, half in disappointment. I opened the envelope, unfolded the sheet of paper inside and read the short, two-sentence message. My face must have registered my incredulity, for when I turned Ashiki was grinning.

'Is this true?'

'I saw with my two eyes,' he said.

'Where?'

'At Good Life.'

'I thought you stopped going there?'

'Yes, for several months. But I went back last night.'

'And you saw her?'

'With my two eyes.'

'It's hard to believe this,' I said, peering back at the note. 'What did she say?'

'About what?'

'Me.'

'Oh, nothing much. Just that she hadn't seen you in a long time.'

After Ashiki left I read the note again.

> I told you in an earlier letter that love was growing inside me. Well, I'm five months pregnant!
>
> Iyese, 9 October

I folded away the letter and left the library. Iyese pregnant! It couldn't be true. There was only one thing to do: return that night to Good Life and see for myself.

◆

At 7:40 that evening I stationed myself under cover of darkness across the street from Good Life. The bar's entrance was dimly lit by two blue bulbs. I followed the flow of men and women in and out of the bar, but an hour later I had not seen Iyese. My eyes ached from all the straining and blinking. Had she slipped in during a moment when my attention had wandered? Or was this one of those rare nights when she decided not to go out?

Suddenly I felt ridiculous, lurking in the shadows like a criminal or a detective. I walked off down the street on the dark side until the sound from the bar became muted. Then I hailed a taxi and went home.

A month later:

> Ashiki gave you my letter, so I know you know I'm pregnant. He told me you're okay, just busy.
>
> Isa came to my flat two days ago. He brought jewellery, shoes, perfume and clothes. I'm keeping them until I see somebody who needs them. He was surprised to see me pregnant. He said he hopes it's a boy, as if that would entitle him to my baby.
>
> There's a favour I want to ask you, but that will be later.
>
> I love you.
Iyese, 14 November.

> If you're counting, you will know it's seven months since we last saw each other. Not once have you thought of writing back, or visiting. Is this who you really are? Was everything between us just a meaningless game? Why did I think there was more of a man in you? I fell in love with the human being I thought I saw inside you. Perhaps you saw only the falling, not the love. A shame!
>
> Iyese, 9 December

> I realise that the tone of my last letter was angry. But I had to be true to my feelings. The past few months have been difficult. I hardly go out these days, not even to Good Life.

And yet, apart from Violet, I have no friends to come around to my flat. I wish you were around to stroke my belly and feel the baby kick.

I know you have chosen a different path. Perhaps you throw my letters into the waste basket, unread. But I will continue to write to you for as long as I wish to.

The baby is due on 15 February, a month from today, but seems to be in a hurry. Already, I feel cramp pains all over my belly. It's worst at night, when it keeps me awake. Yet, I'm happy. Very happy!

Isa came by yesterday. He wanted to know how his baby was doing, he said. His baby! I have not said one word to him yet, which he takes as a sign he has not bought me enough presents for me to forget what happened.

I mentioned in an earlier letter about asking you a favour. I want some photos of you, as many as you can spare. The baby may never meet you, but it would be nice to show him or her pictures of the man who changed my life (then ran away!). I hope you will do this for me. And soon.

I may not write to you again until after the baby is born.

Iyese, 14 January

The first Saturday after the due date, I decided to visit Iyese. The night before, I sorted through my photographs and made a handsome selection. I arranged the twelve pictures in chronological order and placed them in a small polythene bag that also contained a congratulatory card and several small gifts for the baby: soaps, oils and toys – items that would do for a boy or a girl, since I did not know the baby's sex.

The day began with sunshine, but a brisk breeze brought clouds which thickened until the sun was blotted out. As I rode in a taxi to Iyese's flat, the firmament bulged with wetness. Lightning relumed the sky with silvery streaks and thunder grumbled overhead. Then the sky's broken water came down in monstrous sheets. Within minutes the city's open gutters were awash with sediment rubbish. The skins of yams, cocoyams, cassava, oranges, bananas and plantains were borne like dead bodies on the rushing stream.

The storm had not abated when I arrived at Iyese's flat. I dashed from the taxi to her door, the bag of gifts held to my chest. Panting, I knocked on Iyese's door, straining to pick up a response through the swish of tyres on the street and the pattering sound of the rain. After a second louder knock I turned the knob. The door yielded. I took a deep breath and went in.

The room was neatly ordered, nothing out of place. I called out Iyese's name, softly at first, then loudly. Then, my heart pounding, I drew apart the partition that led to her bedroom. Iyese was sprawled on the floor, naked, her baby clutched to her chest. Her eyes were wide open, her mouth agape; a trail of blood ran out across the floor. Paralysed, tongue-tied, I only stared. I thought I saw her move slightly and I blurted out her name, but she remained silent, for the winking of my own eye had created the illusion.

Stepping closer, I saw a gash on the baby's right leg, an ugly knife wound from which blood still flowed. Was the baby also dead or simply asleep?

Afterwards I could not remember how long I had stood, staring. When I snapped out of my trance it was to a feeling of intense fear. What if somebody came in and found me at the scene of this horrible crime? Fetching a washcloth, I wiped my fingerprints off the door knob. Then I tiptoed out of her flat.

The storm had gathered still greater force. I walked in a daze, little caring about the rain, which soaked the photographs and presents in my plastic bag. The screech of tyres on wet tarmac, then the long blast of a car horn startled me. I looked up in time to see a car stop sharply in front of me, hardly a foot between us.

'Bastard!' cursed the driver. *'Akula!* If you're looking for death, go and jump into a latrine!' I stood transfixed, trembling all over. The driver reversed the car, turned the wheels away from me, then drove off, still cursing.

The streets were nearly empty. Yet I felt that many hidden eyes were fixed on me as I walked on through the rain.

Chapter Nineteen

Having eaten little all weekend, I arrived in my office on Monday tired and listless. I had just sat down when my phone rang.

'There's a lady here who wants to see you,' said the female receptionist.

'Her name?'

'She refuses to say.'

'Why?'

'I don't know, but she's been quite rude.'

In the background I heard somebody cursing. 'Na your mama be quite rude! Na you be rude, you hear!' I recognised Violet's voice.

'I'll be there in a second,' I said.

At reception Violet stood akimbo, glowering, her mouth drawn into a contemptuous pout.

'Ah, Violet,' I said, feigning surprise. 'Please come with me.'

I led the way outside.

'Do you want something to drink? There's a bar nearby.'

'I no come to drink. I simply wan' tell you say he done kill Emilia.'

I furrowed my brows as if confounded. 'Who's *he*? What did he do?'

'Isa. Major Bello. He kill Emilia.'

'Iyese is dead?'

'Yes, Emilia done die.'

I gasped. 'Why? How?'

'She jus' tell Isa say na you be the papa of her boy pikin.'

'Wait a minute. She told Isa I was the father of her baby boy?'

'Correct.'

'Why would he kill her for that?'

'Because Isa want boy pikin bad bad.'

I gasped again. 'How can you be sure Major Bello did this?'

'Emilia been plan to do naming ceremony for the pikin last Saturday evening. She tell Isa say na your name she wan' give the pikin. The news vex Isa well well. Na that same Saturday Emilia die. If witch fly for night and person come die, then the witch must to answer.'

'What happened to the baby? Is he dead too?'

'No. The *banza* man stab the pikin, but him no die. Child Welfare take the pikin go hospital. Na me police ask to identify Emilia's dead body. Even self, na me tell Child Welfare the pikin name. After the pikin recover, Welfare plan to send him to Langa Orphanage. If you like, you fit go there see the baby. Emilia tell me say, true true, na you be the pikin papa.'

'I don't think that's likely,' I said.

Violet flared up. 'Why you speak so? You mean to say Emilia lie? You two no sleep together? I been think say you be better man. Now, I know say you be nonsense man, true true.'

No doubt she considered my grief inadequate, and perhaps she was right. Although we were bound by a common loss, our concerns were different. One death, separate memories.

'Iyese did not deserve this,' I said, to break the silence. 'She was such a sweet person.'

Violet continued to look at me in silence, as if my words were insipid compared to the emotions she felt. At last she said, 'I jus' say make I come tell you wetin happen. You be bad man, but I know say Emilia like you too much. More than too much.'

'Did the police ask you any other questions?' I couldn't help worrying about the complications that might arise if the Child Welfare Department looked me up.

'They ask whether me know who killed Emilia. I tell them I no fit to talk. Thas why I say make I come ask you first.'

'I don't think there is any use in accusing Isa,' I suggested. 'The police won't touch him. He's a powerful emir's son. And also an army officer. Besides, the case against him is only circumstantial.' Violet regarded me coldly. 'Thank you for all the trouble you took. The best thing is to let Iyese rest in peace.'

'*Otio!*' she shouted. 'Which kin' peace? Which kin' rest in peace? No, Emilia no fit rest in peace at all at all. She no go rest until bad death come kill Isa. Na that time Emilia fit rest.'

'Well, if Isa did this he will receive his just desserts eventually,' I said.

She looked at me reproachfully. 'I dey go,' she said, already walking away.

Returning to my desk, I sat and brooded. I had the sensation of being in a time warp, trapped in the one unchanging moment when I found Iyese lying dead. I was back in Iyese's room, staring at her bloodied body, her baby on her chest, also spattered with blood. Nothing I did could free my mind from that scene. I feared that I would live all my life shut up in that room, my eyes forever riveted on that horrific sight.

'Your letters, sir.'

The words broke into my consciousness long after the office messenger had spoken them and gone on to deliver mail to other desks. I thumbed through my letters indifferently until I saw an envelope that bore Iyese's handwriting. My heart's ferocious beating was compounded of fear and anticipation. My hands shook as I held the letter up to my face and read:

He looks just like you! Eyes, mouth, forehead – just like you. A happy, handsome little boy! Perhaps a carbon copy of you when you were a baby.

In my last letter I asked you for some photographs. Since I didn't hear from you, I guess your answer is no. That won't stop me telling this baby about the lift you gave my life.

Now, I have another favour to ask you. In two days the baby will be a week old. In my village the seventh day is when the naming ceremony is done. I want to name the baby Ogugua. I hope you won't mind sharing the gift of a name with him.

Will I ever see you again? Have you ever thought about it?

Love,
Iyese

P.S. Isa came around two days ago and asked me to marry him! Can you believe that? I'll look for a new flat for me and the baby. Isa will be dangerous when he realises that I won't let him have this baby.

Again,
Iyese

Ogugua. The name my mother had muttered the very instant I was put in her arms, birth blood hardly dried on my soft, coppery skin. My father had intended to give me another name, but the moment my mother held me in her arms and said Ogugua, he knew that was what I would be called. She had pronounced the word as if it were written on my forehead, inscribed in a language she alone could decipher.

Ogugua – a male name. Yet my father was certain his wife would still have insisted on it even if I had been born a girl. For what mattered to her was what the name meant, the statement she wanted to make to the world. Ogugua, condensed from Oguguamakwa. Literally, the wiper of my tears. My consoler, vindicator and comforter. In my case the name was blighted by a terrible irony. I had wiped my mother's tears, true; but I had also sent her to an early grave.

◆

As time passed my guilt grew less acute; the image of Iyese seemed to fade. Then one day a colleague brought her newborn baby to the office. The baby's penetrating eyes in its tiny, tender, vulnerable face made me think about Iyese all over again. I was tortured with the thought that Iyese's baby might truly be my son, the first of the many children my grandmother had prayed that I should have. I considered going to the orphanage, but in the end fear outweighed curiosity: seeing the baby would wake up feelings I was not confident I could face, would exhume emotions I had buried in a shallow grave.

Yet Isa Palat Bello continued to haunt my mind. He was present in every soldier's face, eyes peering out at me, lustful and ugly. I began to dread the approach of night, for his face would loom up out of the dark. Whenever I heard footsteps behind me I whirled around. I stopped going out at night. When friends complained about this I lied: I had been diagnosed with a rare disease that brought on sudden fainting spells; my doctor had ordered me to rest in bed.

Then, one day, I received an unexpected reprieve; it was reported that Bello was among ten officers on their way to Pakistan for a six-month advanced artillery course. That night I went out to visit some friends. A new drug had worked wonders for me, I told them.

I began to regain my former vitality. Sleeping became less grim.

Chapter Twenty

In late November of 1967 the Stockholm-based Hunger Institute issued its annual World Food Picture, a report that correlated food supply to life expectancy. The report listed thirteen countries as 'disasters in progress'; Madia was sixth on the list. The Institute found that food production in the country had declined by 30 per cent; the birth rate was increasing exponentially, and life expectancy had shrunk from 57, five years earlier, to 52. In an even bleaker prognosis, the report projected that within a decade two-thirds of the children born in Madia would live in 'excruciating poverty' and that people would 'literally drop dead in the streets from acute malnutrition'.

Alarmed by the report, the House of Representatives and the Senate summoned Dr Titus Bato, the Honourable Minister of National Planning and Economic Development, to appear before their joint session on 6 December. Dr Bato had a well-earned reputation as the most arrogant minister in the cabinet. He was awkward in appearance, his stringy body tipped to the left. But he managed a superciliousness that many saw as too obvious a compensation for his unfetching physique. His calling card listed all his degrees and the names of the institutions that awarded them: B.Sc., London School of Economics; M.Sc., Chicago; Ph.D., Columbia.

I arrived at the National Assembly at 11 a.m., an hour before Dr Bato was scheduled to appear. The press gallery was packed. The minister strode into the chamber at 11:56 a.m., his face composed and confident. The Speaker of the House struck the gavel three times on his desk. When the requisite silence had fallen he announced that the session had formally begun.

He began by asking Dr Bato what he thought of the Hunger Institute report.

'It's either useless and untrue or, if true, it's good news,' replied the minister. 'On the whole, I think it is the most incoherent and meaningless economic report I have ever read. And I have read quite a few.' He spoke with the ease of one who, expecting that very question, had rehearsed a seamless response.

'Let's take the first part of your answer, Honourable Minister. You said the report may be useless and untrue. Why?'

'Because I have yet to hear of any person in this country scavenging for food in refuse dumps. Therefore, the claim that Madians are starving sounds far-fetched.'

The response provoked suppressed agitation in the chamber, and when the Speaker asked a second question the calm in his voice seemed strained.

'Why would the Institute lie about this country's food situation?'

'Only the Institute can answer that question. I'm here as a representative of the government of Madia.'

'I know who you represent!' the Speaker retorted in a raised voice. 'You have asserted that these people lied in their report. I thought you might share with us the grounds for your conclusion.'

'Correction, Mr Speaker. I have not reached any conclusions. Perhaps you should speak less and listen more closely.'

The Speaker fixed the minister with an icy stare. 'A remark like that constitutes contempt. Be mindful, Honourable Minister, of the rules of conduct in this chamber!'

Dr Bato returned his gaze with an expression nothing short of insolent, and the Speaker, unable to go on questioning calmly, turned to the President of the Senate and, with a slight nod, indicated that he was yielding the floor.

Chief Willy Wakka, the Senate President, was a stout man with a thug's temper but a lawyer's tongue. He cleared his throat.

'Honourable Minister, you have averred that in the event that the report under consideration is an accurate reflection of the facts you would regard it as good news. May I invite you to explain this rather startling view?'

'It is not hard to understand. The Hunger Institute claims that the food crisis will lead to a dramatic rise in the death rate in Madia. It also claims that there has been an explosion in the birth rate in recent years. The total picture is therefore that the death rate will cancel out the birth rate, thus preserving the standard of living. Even children who understand simple arithmetic can follow that logic. It is simple Malthusian economics.'

'Your considered submission, then, is that death is good?'

'I am putting forward the view that death is nature's way of preserving a stable quality of life in any given society.'

'You're not appalled at the prospect of poor Madians dying in large numbers?'

'Why would I be? No, I'm not.'

The unrest that had been building up in the chamber now threatened to overflow. Many law-makers spoke at once, calling for the minister's immediate apology and resignation. Dr Bato sat unmoved, his chin tucked in the palm of his hand, like a professor whose class had turned unaccountably rowdy. The voice of the Speaker shouting 'Order! Order!' rose above the din, but did nothing to quell the pandemonium. Eventually he mounted his desk, stamping his feet and waving his hand. By this desperate measure he finally obtained silence. He spoke in a raised quavering voice.

'The good people of Madia have been insulted. I ask – in exercise of the power vested in me as Speaker of the House of Representatives and Chairman of the Joint Conference – I demand that the Honourable Minister of National Planning and Economic Development tender an immediate apology to Parliament and to the good people of this country.'

An eerie silence fell on the chamber. Everybody waited, parliamentarians and spectators alike. Photographers clicked away in a frenzy, anxious to capture the minister's moment of capitulation.

'I'm not apologising for anything I've said here today. I reaffirm my comments. Nor do I intend to resign. I was not appointed by Parliament and I don't believe I hold my office at your behest.'

One legislator jumped up and moved menacingly towards Dr Bato. Two parliamentary security guards rushed in and stood between him and his target. Four other security guards then escorted the minister out of the chamber amid curses and threats and salvoes of spit.

The next day university students and labour unions called for nation-wide strikes and daily demonstrations until the minister was fired. Instead, Prime Minister Askia Amin went on national television and described Dr Bato as a national asset, 'a man respected by the centres of world finance from New York to Paris'. The prime minister then warned that further demonstrations and disturbances of the peace would be severely dealt with.

One week later students of the National University massed in the football field carrying anti-Bato placards. Three lorryloads of anti-riot police arrived and ordered the students to disperse. A few students walked away, but most of them stayed behind, defiant. The police put on their gear and advanced. They threw a few tear-gas canisters at the students. The students gathered the smoking cans and lobbed them back at the police. The police launched an overwhelming arsenal of tear gas which sent the students scattering, eyes streaming. Then the police released a rattle of machine-gun fire.

Eyewitness accounts estimated that between twenty and thirty corpses were taken away in two police trucks. But in a short statement, the government insisted that 'only four hooligans posing as students were killed'.

People began to speak of the 'Bato Massacre'. Why, Madians asked, did so many young lives have to be sacrificed so that Dr Bato could remain in office and fart in people's faces? As the protests grew, Amin gathered his ministers and top aides and withdrew with them to the Presidential Lodge, a secluded fortress built on a small island, to consider his next move.

The goverment-owned Radio Madia began to broadcast a barrage of propaganda. Listening to the radio's 7 p.m. newscast became a national obsession, as with each passing day the claims made by Madia's leaders became more fantastic. They spoke of polls in which 99.9 per cent of Madians expressed their loyalty to Askia Amin's administration; of rallies in cities all over the country attended by hundreds of thousands of pro-Amin supporters. They asserted that the detained labour and student leaders, moved to shame by their unpatriotic perfidy, had confessed to being paid lackeys of unnamed Western nations intent on thwarting Madia's march to progress. They quoted from 'authoritative studies' indicating a dramatic rise in the people's standard of living. They assured Madians that their leaders were spending sleepless nights over an economic plan that would make the country and its people the envy of other nations on the continent, nay the world.

Such blatant untruths provoked a bizarre reaction: laughter. Women laughed suckling their babies on sapped breasts. The vanquished and famished who craved the comforts of the grave laughed. Madians laughed in groups gathered round their radio sets; they laughed when they met in the street; they laughed in their workplaces and in the markets; they laughed themselves to sleep. There was no gaiety in this laughter: it was compounded of their blood, their sweat, their tears.

On the morning of 1 January 1968 – the ninth day since the prime minister and his cabinet retired to the Presidential Lodge – I turned on the radio, curious to hear what Amin would say in his customary New Year's Day address to the nation. Instead of the national anthem that traditionally preceded the prime minister's speech, the station blared a strange funereal music, its notes sharp and piercing, its syncopation too swift. The music reminded me of the scores that, in horror movies, foreshadowed the vampire's bloody lurch.

A voice came on the radio, rough and shaky, like a nervous drunk's.

Fellow countrymen and women,
This is Major James Rada of the 82nd Armoured Division of the Madian Army. On behalf of the Armed Forces of Madia, I inform you that a change has been made in the leadership of our country. With immediate effect, Prime Minister Askia Amin has been removed as head of the government, the Parliament has been disbanded and all existing political institutions at the local and state levels have been dissolved. All political parties will henceforth cease to exist. All local government officials are hereby directed to report to the police station nearest to them. With immediate effect all national authority will reside with the Armed Forces Revolutionary and Redemptive Council.
The prime minister and most members of his cabinet have been placed under arrest pending possible prosecution

192

on charges of contributing to the economic adversity and political turmoil of the Federal Republic of Madia.

Fellow citizens, we have all been witnesses to the escalating acts of irresponsibility and corruption exhibited by the political classes. The ordinary citizen has lost all confidence in the institutions of governance; the state and national treasuries have been bankrupted by politicians for their own profit; and the moral fabric of this nation has been torn apart.

The Armed Forces of Madia have watched with increasing sadness and anxiety as the situation developed to crisis point. It was with the greatest reluctance but out of a sense of patriotic duty that we decided to seize the reins of power in order to avert any further deterioration.

Anybody, or group of people, who in any way challenges the authority of the Armed Forces Revolutionary and Redemptive Council will be summarily dealt with. Fellow countrymen and women, you are advised to stay tuned and await further announcements and instructions. Long live the Federal Republic of Madia.

Thank you.

At the end of the broadcast I found that my palms were sweaty, a formless fear awhirl in my head. I took a long cold bath. Then I put on a black T-shirt over a pair of jeans and set out to my office.

The streets were jammed. Cars blasted their horns. People embraced one another and pumped hands. Jubilant crowds chanted, 'Hang Amin!', 'Askia is axed!', 'Down with Amin's corruption!', 'Welcome AFRRC!'. Those who had not heard the broadcast huddled around any available radio set and listened to the martial music while waiting for the announcement to be repeated. Every half-hour there was a pause in the music, then the station re-broadcast Major Rada's speech. I loathed the people's uncomplicated reaction, the crowd's certitude that the current development portended good. Was I alone in detecting a presentiment of terror in the officer's tone? Was I the only one who foresaw that the coup would entail much spilling of Madian blood?

◆

The newsroom was in a frenzied state. The chatter of reporters rose and fell against the constant clatter of typewriters. At one point in the morning one of our photographers staggered in, dripping blood, the right side of his head swollen. Shakily he told us how a group of soldiers had beaten him at a checkpoint, upset that he had taken their picture.

'What was wrong with taking their picture?' asked the news editor.

'They said I had contravened national security.'

'How? What national security?' queried the editor.

The photographer spread his hands in an uncomprehending gesture.

'Didn't you tell them you were from the press?'

'I did. I showed them my I.D.'

'And then?'

'One of them snatched it from me. Then he took out a jackknife and cut my card to pieces. He said I was a spy. They started punching and kicking me and beating me with the butts of their guns.'

'Guns?'

'Yes, their guns and fists at the same time. They threatened to take me to their barracks and shoot me right away. But then an officer appeared on the scene and ordered them to release me.

He asked them to return my camera, but they had already exposed the film.'

'Take a taxi to the clinic and get yourself seen to. Then take two days off. As soon as the situation stabilises we'll take the matter up with the appropriate authorities.'

The photographer thanked the editor and limped away. When he was out of sight the news editor turned to me.

'These people are not allowed to bully innocent citizens.'

'Yes they are,' I said bitterly. 'They have guns. And they now run this country.'

◆

That night the photographer died in his sleep. His death provided a focus for my disparate feelings about the coup. I thought again about the people celebrating out in the streets, like children welcoming a first rainfall after a long, hard dry season. It all reminded me of a story my grandmother once told me, about the ambivalent character of rain, sustainer of the earth's plenitude but also the harbinger of malaise.

Once upon a time, a great famine struck a remote village that was located beyond seven seas and seven wilds. The famine was caused by several years of drought that made the earth too hard to till. Horrified by the rate at which their fellows died, the villagers consulted a *dibia* to find out the source of their affliction. The diviner said that a sacrifice must be carried to the boundary between earth and sky. The errand must be performed by a creature nimble of foot and ample-voiced, for the journey was far and the sky was hard of hearing.

The villagers decided to send Dog. They instructed him to hasten without distraction. But Dog strayed off many times. He sniffed the air for game, joined a group of hunters he met in the forest, tarried to watch a wrestling match, traded wits with Tortoise, sang with a travelling choir of birds, danced with a troupe of gazelles. By the time he eventually arrived at the boundary, the sky had drifted off, sullen. Dog barked and barked until the sky returned.

'Here,' said Dog in a contemptuous voice. 'Here is your sacrifice. Now send rain to the poor villagers!' He flung the sacrifice on the ground and turned home, looking forward to all the stops he would make on his way back to the village.

Weeks later he reached the village to find it flooded. The villagers were all dead, their corpses afloat in pools of water. It had been raining relentlessly since the day Dog insulted the sky.

'Rain has two faces,' concluded my grandmother. 'It can give life, but its arrows can also cause death.'

Arrows of rain: my grandmother's phrase for rain's malefic face.

◆

Late in the afternoon of the day of the coup, a reporter known for his scoops walked in and announced that he had spoken to one of the soldiers who arrested Prime Minister Amin at 2:15 a.m. Everybody abandoned their tasks and crowded around him to hear his account.

When they stormed the Presidential Lodge, the soldiers had little trouble rounding up most of their targets. The ministers and political aides sat or lay in the expansive Congress Hall where cabinet meetings were held, some of them still awake, but all hopelessly drunk. Some were naked, drained by the exhaustion of love. Two or three members of the Power Platoon attended to each minister. The officials and their women were quickly arrested and marched outside and into a truck.

Another group of soldiers paced the corridors of the Lodge looking for the prime minister. They threw doors open, peered into closets, checked under beds, searched everywhere. They ransacked two floors but found no sign of Amin. The officer in charge then ordered his men to follow him to the underground level. Approaching the first door, they heard ardent voices coming from the room beyond. Pausing to listen, they heard a man breathlessly saying, 'Tell me when to come.' Then there was a woman's voice: 'Now, Your Excellency. Come Tiger! Come Champion! Come Emperor! Now!'

The officer pushed open the door and walked into the room followed by eight soldiers. Their entrance attracted the prime minister's notice. He looked up and halted his thrusts, but the girl under him still wriggled her hips, too far consumed by love's heady thrill. The prime minister's eyes narrowed in indignation at the sight of the intruders. The officer came to attention and executed a brisk salute that was at once deferential and contemptuous.

'Mr Prime Minister, Sir, I have instructions to effect your arrest!'

For a moment the prime minister seemed to struggle with incomprehension. Then, hit by the fact of his nakedness, he pulled the bed covers over his buttocks. In a voice that carried all the authority he could muster in the circumstances, he asked, 'Who in this country has issued such instructions?'

'The AFRRC.'

'The AF what?' he enquired with fierce impatience.

'Armed Forces Revolutionary and Redemptive Council, Sir.'

'Impossible! There's no such council.'

'Yes, there has been a coup. Your government has been removed.'

'Impossible! The people elected me. Nobody can remove me. Go and tell your revolutionary council to stand election if they want power. And by the way, protocol demands that you should address me as Your Excellency.'

'Your Excellency, I would not try to resist arrest if I were you.'

The prime minister slowly lifted himself off the girl, who seemed for the first time to recognise the awkwardness of lying in bed with a man who was losing power. Amin sat down at the edge of the bed, looked sternly at the soldiers and sighed. Then he muttered, 'Only bastards would interrupt an orgasm!'

The soldiers chuckled. Their derision seemed to bring home to the prime minister the reality of his fall. Amin asked the officer for permission to make a call to the Army Chief of Staff.

The officer's tone was curt. 'He's dead.'

'What!' cried Askia Amin.

'He was court-martialled two hours ago for colluding with your government against the interests of the Madian people.'

'What!'

'He was found guilty and was executed along with other corrupt officers in the Navy and Air Force.'

'What!'

'And even if he were still alive you wouldn't be able to speak to him. Telephone communication was shut off when this operation began five hours ago.'

Amin pulled on his trousers. He was about to put on a shirt when the officer stopped him. 'A shirt is not allowed.'

'Why not?'

'These are my instructions,' said the officer.

In a voice now full of fear Amin asked, 'What are you planning to do with me?'

'I don't know,' answered the officer. 'It's in the hands of the AFRRC.'

'Gentlemen, I'll give you one million dollars if you let me escape.'

The officer shook his head.

'I'll make it two million. In cash.'

One of the soldiers stepped forward with handcuffs. The prime minister pleaded with desperation.

'Five million dollars, gentlemen. If you let me go. You can say you couldn't find me. Please!'

The officer laughed. 'For the last time I ask you to cooperate with us to avoid injury to yourself.'

Trembling, Amin allowed them to put on the manacles. Another soldier produced handcuffs for his girlfriend.

'I did nothing,' she said, sobbing. 'He forced me. Please, I'm too young to die.'

'Calm down,' the officer told her. 'Nobody is going to shoot you. You'll testify against him, that's all.' Then, as an afterthought, he addressed Amin. 'Sir, about what the AFRRC might do with you. I want you to know that castration is definitely an option.'

The soldiers sniggered. In a last defiant gesture, Askia Amin lifted his face and looked into the officer's eyes. Then he spat at the officer's feet. The soldier who had put the handcuffs on him marched forward and slapped him twice on the face.

◆

In the days that followed, Askia Amin and his ministers were arraigned before a special military tribunal. The trial became a carnival. Crowds thronged outside the building, chanting alleluias to the military redeemers and demanding death for Amin and his gang.

In the event the tribunal was lenient. Amin was sentenced to two life terms in prison, the cabinet members to one life term each.

Chapter Twenty-one

A day after the coup Major James Rada returned on Radio Madia and announced that Major Isa Palat Bello, just selected as the new head of state and commander-in-chief of the Madian armed forces, was about to address the nation. Hearing Bello's name, I had the fleeting urge to laugh. Certainly, I thought, someone at Radio Madia had decided to make a ghastly joke at my expense.

The national anthem came on, dispelling my doubts. Then I heard Bello's familiar hoarse voice.

Beloved fellow countrymen and women. Today marks an important epoch in the chequered history of our great nation . . .

My throat tightened and my head seemed to spin. 'Murderer!' I cried.

The moral turpitude of the deposed government . . . their unbridled rape of the Madian people . . . financial recklessness and social anarchy . . . We now have a great opportunity for national economic and moral renewal . . .

For a while, my mind tuned in and out, dimly grasping Bello's words. Then a cold fear crept up inside me and I was transported to the past, to the fount of terrible memories. I remembered Iyese pinned against the wall with Bello's hand at her throat. The two pillows basted with her blood. The grotesque tranquillity of her final posture, stretched out with her baby on her breast.

Bello's voice broke in again. *The government is firmly deter-*

mined to deal summarily with any trouble makers . . . Terrors I could neither name nor disentangle dinned in my head. This man whose cruelty I knew so intimately now personified absolute power. And I was his enemy!

Throughout the night my body twitched, my teeth chattered. I slept only in short spurts, my rest haunted by bad dreams. The next morning there were pictures of Bello everywhere: on billboards and in shop windows, on every newspaper's front page. Soldiers milled around the city, guns strung across their chests. Their gaze seemed to single me out and follow me. I began to avoid the streets.

One morning I woke up after a nightmarish sleep and called my office. The receptionist told me that two men had been in to see me. They had not left their names, only the message that they would return. No, she had never seen the men before. 'Thank you,' I said in a voice choked with dread. 'Put me through to the editor.'

I told the editor that I was very sick, that when I stood up the world seemed to spin around me. I had no need to see a doctor, I assured him; this thing had happened to me twice before. It was a sort of psychic exhaustion triggered by a rare chemical imbalance that could not be controlled with drugs. The doctor who diagnosed it several years ago had said that all I needed was to stay in bed for a few days, listen to soothing music, eat once a day (and only vegetables) and drink lots of water – nothing carbonated.

I talked without pausing, afraid that the editor might ask a question that would expose my lies, or say that he knew such and such a doctor I ought to see. Then I came to my point.

'I was wondering if I could take a week off. To rest in bed. I was told that if I didn't get proper rest I could easily have seizures. Bad ones, or even a stroke.'

He was silent for a moment. Had he found a hole in my story? I waited, tense.

'Bloody hell,' he finally said, in his accustomed fashion. 'Take two weeks.'

I gripped the handset of the phone, hardly believing my luck. For two weeks, I thought, I would be out of circulation, hidden away from the soldiers' stabbing eyes. In my relief I did not consider the possibility that the new solitude could birth its own monsters.

At midnight I got into bed to sleep. The instant I shut my eyes the image of Major Bello stood over me, his gun aimed at the ridge of my nose. Lying on my back, I peered straight into the gun's muzzle, dark and small. I struggled hard to erase this image from my mind. In its place came a fluttering sound and a ghost draped in a mauve veil, hovering over me. Slowly, the veil turned a dark red, became a cloud of blood, then dripped all over my bed. I watched with dread as the ghost's form became clearer and more familiar.

'Iyese!' I shouted, jerking myself upright with a nervous impetus. The ghost was gone, merged into the opaque fabric of the night. I was alone, a heaving, terrified man.

'Iyese,' I whispered. The room was eerily quiet. I touched my bed, a pool of sweat. I turned on the light. The time was 1:03 a.m. I reached for the phone and dialled. Ola Jones, a friend from my university days, answered after seven rings. His speech was slurred with sleep. I told him who it was. 'This better be important,' he warned, 'or I'll kill somebody!'

'My life's in danger. I must come over to your house. Immediately.'

'Can't you wait till the morning?'

'No. I don't know what might happen. It may be too late.'

'Have you called the police?'

'No.'

'Do.'

'I can't.'

'You can't? Why not?'

'I'll tell you when I get there.'

'There's a curfew in effect, you know. What if you get arrested for breaking it?'

'Your home is only two miles away. I can manage.'

'Tell me, you're not running from the law, are you?'

'I'll tell you when I get there . . .'

'Because I don't want to harbour a fugitive.'

'When I get there.'

The streets were empty. In the days before the coup, a few cars would have been about. There would be a number of Hausa retailers at their *suya* stands, selling a variety of peppered meat to an unending procession of nocturnal customers. But that night Langa was a dead city, its residents confined indoors.

I took a back street and walked stealthily, ready to duck at the slightest suggestion of danger. It was not long before I reached Ola's house. There were lights on in his living room. I tapped lightly on the door. A woman I did not know let me in. I was not surprised: at university Ola was nicknamed *uchichi agba aka* because there was no night when he did not sleep with some woman. Stepping into the room, I saw Ola on the couch, his face covered with a magazine. He had no doubt asked his woman to open the door so that I would get the message that I had disturbed more than his sleep. Such an unsubtle bastard, I thought. He got up when I walked into the room, smiling radiantly, charming as ever.

'Young man!' he bellowed, hugging me. He always addressed me that way even though I was a full two years older than he.

'Sit down. Guinness stout or will it be brandy?' He stopped short, narrowed his eyes with intensity, and inspected my face.

'Young man, you've grown old on me. What are these stress marks doing around your eyes? Are you sick? Has the job been too demanding? Are you getting enough sleep? Tell me, what's really going on?'

I glanced briefly in the direction of his girlfriend.

'Go on to bed, Angela,' he said to her. 'We'll be fine.'

'I'm not sleepy.'

'That's okay. Just wait in bed then. I'll join you.'

'When?'

'Soon as I finish talking with this young man here.'

'What if the talk takes all night?'

'Then it takes all night!' Ola snapped.

'I don't even know why you woke me up in the first place,' she grumbled. Presently she slammed shut the bedroom door.

'Yes, young man. Who's threatening your life?'

'Isa Palat Bello.'

'The new head of state?'

I nodded.

'Did you write anything against his regime?'

I shook my head.

'I didn't think so. So why do you think he's after you?'

'He's a rapist and a murderer.'

'Wait a minute now! The man has been in power for what? – a few days. And already you accuse him of rape and murder. I didn't suspect you were one of those idealists who think a corrupt elected government is better than a corrective military regime. Major Bello intervened to save this country from Amin and his cabal of thieves. Idealists like you must face reality. Let's give the military a chance to clean up the mess.'

'You don't understand,' I said.

'No, *you* don't understand. This is a clear case of wrong-headed idealism. Who could this man have raped in one week?'

'He really did rape a woman. And killed her. Not since becoming head of state; before. Two years ago.'

'Who found out that he did this?'

'I.'

'Did you report this to the police or write about it?'

'No.'

'You don't expect me to take you seriously, do you?'

'I knew the victim. She was his girlfriend. Well, sort of.'

'His girlfriend? How does one rape one's girlfriend?'

'In his case quite savagely. Then when she had a baby son and refused to acknowledge him as the father, he murdered her too. Viciously.'

Ola mulled this over for a moment. 'Don't think I make light of your story,' he said. 'But look at things this way. According to you, Bello raped and murdered this woman you knew. You didn't take the story to the police nor did you write about it. Why then would Bello want to harm you?'

'Because I know how he looks when he isn't wearing a mask.'

'You're the least of Bello's problems. He's now a head of state.'

'And a commander in chief,' I added. 'That's precisely my point. He always had a motive to silence me. Now he has the power, too. Besides, two strangers went to the newspaper looking for me. Tell me they're not Bello's security operatives.'

'I can tell you that. I'm sure this was not the first time strangers called in at the office to see you. The head of state isn't going to lose sleep thinking how to deal with – don't take this the wrong way – a common journalist. He's got a country to run.'

He yawned and looked at his watch, then popped open his eyes in alarm.

'4:10! It's the first time I've been up this late without a beautiful woman having something to do with it. Young man, let's resume our talks later today. It's Angela's first visit, so I must make a good impression. Good night.'

◆

I spent four days in Ola's house. My second day in hiding Radio Madia announced that the new regime had lifted the curfew. All air and sea ports were reopened; telephone services, which had been restored locally two days after the coup, were now restored for international calls. The station also announced the promotion of several members of the junta. Major Bello was made a major general by special 'accelerated promotion'.

I stayed awake each night, holed up in the dingy room where Ola dumped his dirty clothes. I read books and drank brandy and had wide-eyed dreams in which terror appeared in all guises. In my solitude I began to hold conversations with myself. On the third day Ola eased open the door and entered the room, intruding on one such session.

'Why is your voice so high?' he asked. I froze and gazed at him. His face had an expression of puzzlement and mild fright.

'I'm meeting some of the gang for drinks at the Metropolitan Club this evening. Eze will be there. And Ahmed, Tunde, and, of course, Ada. Probably George too. I'm sure they'd all like to see you.'

'No,' I said.

'No what?'

'I'm not coming.'

He turned sharply and left the room.

Later that night, while I lay in bed reading, Ola returned, all four friends in tow. They barged into my room, nattering, their faces overspread with drunken smiles.

'How was the evening?' I asked.

'Splendid, in spite of you!' said Ada, the only woman in the group. She came over to see what I was reading. It was Albert Camus's *The Plague*. 'So reading a sick book is more important than drinking with the gang?'

At the university we had all belonged to a group called PFD, for Politician, Fish, Dog. Our pledge was to throw parties without just cause like politicians, to drink at every opportunity like fish and to have sex with the shamelessness of dogs. After we left the university, I had wandered away from the group and its frivolities, inventing excuses to avoid their wild parties and weekend binges.

Ada was the gang's most enthusiastic member. Her father was a wealthy lawyer who enjoyed huge perks from the numerous multinational corporations on whose boards he sat. She was a tall woman, not pretty but attractive. Some of her comeliness smacked of something paid for with her father's cash: the expensive clothes she wore, the soft sheen of her make-up, the waft of perfume her body gave off. She was complaisant when it came to sex, a woman who seized the slightest opportunity to slip into a man's bed. She drank with abandon (but never became drunk), and she spared no expense when she threw parties.

'I've not been feeling well,' I said. 'My stomach is a little disturbed.'

'That's not what we heard,' said Eze the Loud Mouth. 'We hear you're a man on the run.'

'Yes, but that had nothing to do with it,' I insisted.

'Tell me,' he asked. 'Is it true that General Bello is looking for you to kill?'

'I'm certain of it.' The response shocked them into a momentary silence.

Then Eze, finding his voice, asked, 'Why? Did you sleep with his wife? Or his mother?' They all burst into throaty laughs. I glared at them: the freedom of their laughter was insufferable. I buried my face in *The Plague*.

'We're now too foolish for you to talk to?' asked Ada.

'Your fears are baseless,' Eze said in a strident tone. 'Bello hasn't done one wrong thing. Not one! You should come out of hiding and go back to work.' In a lower voice he went on, 'Listen to me, my friend.' I stopped reading and set my eyes on him. 'Bello is not a murderer. He's a redeemer. All this fear is within you. If you want to see a psychiatrist, we'll help find one. A very good one.'

'You think I'm crazy, then?' I asked.

They made no answer in words, but I read it on their faces, in their eyes.

'Think about Ola's situation,' Eze added. 'He's inconvenienced himself to put you up for a few days. Imagine what would happen to him if – God forbid – General Bello were really out to get you and Ola was caught sheltering you.' He paused to let his point sink in. 'You really should see a psychiatrist. And go back to your home. Nobody is going to harm you.'

◆

Very early the next morning I gathered my clothes into a bundle wrapped in a blanket, then slipped out of the house before Ola woke up. The streets wore a dull, indistinct face, the houses obscured by the morning mist. I had no destination in mind when I began my journey. But as the mist lifted and the sun broke through, the clouds in my mind cleared away and I saw where I was going. I had a vision of sand, sea, sunshine, and endless sky. My path was leading me into exile on the outer edges of life, in the haven of B. Beach.

209

Chapter Twenty-two

From this cell thick with the odour of death, my mind drifts back to the lost years on B. Beach. Certain memories are resurrected: the first few weeks of my exile, the last few before my arrest. Much of the rest of that time is blurred, as if the events of those years have slipped beyond the reach of memory into a vast oblivion.

In the first days on B. Beach my fear was raw, on the surface. At night, the sound of the ocean made me shiver. I carried a cudgel, afraid of what might lurk in the dark. Many times, sensing a motion close by, I swung the cudgel against an imaginary enemy.

Sometimes I ached for my former life and considered returning – moving back into my apartment, presenting myself at the office in the hope that no one had been appointed to my desk. It was a ridiculous dream: the door back to that other world had snapped shut never to be prised open again.

For the first three days I went entirely without food. Hunger seared my hollow belly. By the fourth day the pangs had become unbearable. I shut my eyes and bit into a half-eaten sandwich somebody had tossed away. The next day I found some more discarded food. The meat was a little high, so I swallowed it without chewing.

The sixth day, as I walked along the shoreline, I came to a huge boulder, a relic from the days when convicted armed robbers were executed on the beach. Having endured five nights without shelter, I decided to make this granite cairn my refuge. On nights when the air was cold, I leaned on the boulder and let my body draw warmth from the rock.

Other nights, as soon as the bell at St Gregory's Cathedral chimed midnight, I began my walking routine. Starting off from the boulder, I walked the two and a half miles to what was known as the European section, close to the washed-up carcass of a ship's hull. There, I entered one of the sheds made by local entrepreneurs from bamboo stems and raffia fronds and rented out in the day to white clients wary of the sun. I rested until the bell tolled another hour; then I walked back to the boulder. The going to and fro continued till daybreak – a way of passing sleepless nights. When the night was hot, I walked within reach of the waves, letting the foamy water curl and play around my bare feet, relishing the droplets of spray that settled on my body like tiny, weightless darts.

Moonlit nights held a special magic. The face of the moon floated on the ocean's surface, seeming to sway to some silent but intoxicating music. I grew to love gazing at the night sky, an interminable star-strewn space in which I could lose myself and become invisible.

◆

Six months after Bello's ascension to power, newspapers reported that ten army officers, including Major-General James Rada, had been found guilty of treason and executed. Reading the story, I wondered how much of Madia's misbegotten history could be traced to my silence about Iyese's death.

More such stories reached me through the BBC's broadcasts, which I received on a portable short-wave radio someone left behind on the beach. I also read numerous accounts in the foreign newspapers discarded by diplomats. The headlines said it all:

MADIAN WRITER HANGED – He was a critic of the
  dictatorship
MADIAN MINISTER'S DEATH SUSPICIOUS – Dictator said
  to be having an affair with deceased's wife
120 STUDENT PROTESTERS REPORTED KILLED
DESPOT CANES VICE-CHANCELLOR IN PUBLIC
DIPLOMATS SAY AFRICAN DICTATOR BEHIND
  DISAPPEARANCE OF OPPONENTS – Victims may have
  been fed to lions

Each headline was a reproach to me for my cowardice. Why
had I not mustered the courage to tell Iyese's story long ago,
when it might have made a difference?

The underground opposition press painted a picture that was
even more grim: countless men picked up and tortured for saying
a bad word about Bello in an unguarded moment in some bar;
women, too, detained and tortured; children orphaned by assassins. Bello's rapaciousness had catapulted him to the front ranks
of the world's wealthiest potentates, behind the Emir of Brunei,
but ahead of Zaire's quick-fingered man-god.

It was impossible to avoid the conclusion that with Madia in
such hands, I was better off living as I was. With time I felt less
involved in my country's plight or the history that had led up to
it. The past seemed to recede further and further from my
thoughts. My nights became more peaceful. Now and again I
even managed to sleep. I was confident that nothing from my
past would ever trouble my quiet life.

◆

One night last September a woman's shrieks rent the air. I froze,
my whole body compelled to listen. More screams came, shriller.
Goose bumps rose all over my skin. A crescent moon hung in

213

the sky, its reflection shifting with the waves. By the moon's pale light I saw the dim shapes of several figures. I crouched down on the wet sand and began to observe their motions.

One after another, the figures cast off their clothes, then dropped to the ground. At first I thought there was only one woman. Then I heard another piercing gasp, the sound a woman makes when the flesh of her sex is torn. A third woman joined in. Perhaps she was younger than the first two, or else more broken by the tearing of her tissue. Her sound was a low, sustained wail.

Drunken male voices wove in and out of the women's cries. The men shouted, threatened, cajoled, laughed. In time the female voices quietened to muffled moans, but the men kept up their lascivious energy. Two hours later, finally sated, the men put their clothes back on and made off in a military truck.

The women lay on the sand, not making a sound. An hour passed. Then, certain that the soldiers would not return, I stood up and went towards the spot where the women lay. On seeing me, two of them sprang to their feet and ran away, scrambling into their tattered clothes. But one lay still, her torn garments scattered about her. Kneeling beside her, I looked into her face. Her eyes were shut, her cheeks drawn down in an attitude of pain.

'Can you hear me?' I murmured.

Her body shook with a spasm of dread. She half-opened one eye and dully took me in. I burrowed my hands under her body. As I lifted, her weight dragged down my arms, heavy like a corpse. I manoeuvred her on to my shoulder and gathered up what remained of her clothes. Then I trudged with her towards the waves.

A faint sun was already peeping out of the sky when she regained consciousness. Attempting to raise herself up on her elbows, she winced with pain and fell back on the sand.

'Are you okay?' Responding to the gentleness of my voice,

she told me what had happened. Her name was Tay Tay. She was a prostitute. 'But not,' she said, 'a real prostitute.' Her voice was low, like one muttering something improbable to herself. I was silent, not wishing to intrude into the dialogue she was having with her soul.

'I am not like Lovet and Tina,' she said. She turned her head towards me. 'What happened to them?'

'The ones who were with you?'

She flicked her eyelid in response.

'They ran away when they saw me,' I replied.

She grunted and shut her eyes. I read the details of her face, the child-like amplitude of her cheeks, the clean line of her nose, the arc of her forehead, her upper lip, projected outward, like a sulker's. The thought that she was Iyese, wearing the body of another woman, visiting me from the past, filled me with an urge to leave her. I resisted the urge to run away from this woman I had brought back from the dead.

'I am not like Tina and Lovet,' she repeated.

'I know,' I said.

'I don't like standing beside the road,' she said. 'Tina and Lovet go out every night. I join them only when things are hard. For one night; at most two. Just to make quick money.' The heaving of her breasts drew my eyes to the imprints of her attackers' hands, their scratches and teeth marks. She gritted her teeth and paused.

'I heard your screams,' I said. 'And I saw the soldiers. What did they do to you?'

A line of tears streaked down the side of her face.

'Who are you?' she asked.

'I don't know any more.'

She regarded me with sorrowful interest. 'I sometimes feel the same way. I am lost in an endless dream and I can't remember my name. Or my face.'

'In my case, it's what I remember that reminds me that I am lost.'

'Tell me why you helped me,' she demanded.

'Again, I don't know. Maybe I was trying to save myself. From my past. But I want to know about *you*. Tell me what they did to you.'

She covered her face with her hands and began to cry. I saw a cut on her left arm, swollen and caked with blood.

'We stood at the Ojuelegba bus stop, looking for customers. That's where we usually stand. Tina and Lovet stand there every night. Myself only when things are hard. Suddenly, there was a big commotion. People scattered in every direction. Tina and Lovet and myself thought armed robbers were raiding the bus stop again. So we stood still because it's not good to panic when there's confusion. We know a woman who ran without looking and landed in the hands of the robbers. They made her eyes see pepper.

'By the time we saw the army people, it was too late to run. At least ten of them surrounded us. One of them pointed his gun at us and shouted, "Freeze or you're dead!" They slapped us, *twap! twap!* Stars flew from my eyes. Blood filled my mouth. I was so afraid of losing it that I swallowed it. The soldiers made us jump like frogs to where their trucks were parked. There were three trucks in all, and they arrested seven girls.

'One of the girls kept shouting that she was not a prostitute. The commander of the troops slapped her until she collapsed. Then he stood over her. Smiling, he said, "If you are not a prostitute, that means you're fresh meat. That's the kind I like. I will make you a prostitute tonight." '

Her voice trailed off and her breath came in gasps as she relived the dreadful memory.

'The soldiers put Tina, Lovet and me in one truck. Five

soldiers were in the back with us. They smelled of *ogogoro* and *wee wee*. They called us bushmeat and boasted how they would show us "army fire". Until the truck stopped here, we didn't know where they were taking us.'

She strained against the glare of the sun and looked into my eyes, as if to say that I knew the rest of the story.

Silence enveloped us. Looking out to the waves, I thought about her story and about Iyese. The past seemed to intermix with the present. Iyese's image, dulled by time, regained clarity. I remembered the emptied look in Iyese's eyes the day she was raped. My flight from her. Her letters to me, full of hopeless longing and mild reproach. Then her murder on a day arrows of rain pelted the earth.

Tay Tay stared at me, perhaps wondering what I thought about her, now that she had unmasked herself to me. How I judged her in her nakedness. Little did she know that a man such as I could not judge anybody.

'How many of them raped you?' I asked.

She let out a burst of laughter. 'How do you expect me to know that? After the first two, I stopped counting. It could have been one soldier tearing my thighs apart. Or all the soldiers in the world. What does it matter? The pain was the same. It was . . . There's no way to describe it.'

'I am sorry,' I said.

Chapter Twenty-three

I had lived on B. Beach for close to twenty years when the screams of Tay Tay and the others awoke the demons of my past. After that the hallucinations about knives and shadowy men with guns resumed, along with the old insomnia. I kept my ears open at night because I had promised Tay Tay that the next time I heard a woman scream I would walk up to the soldiers and spoil their gruesome party, even at the risk of my life.

For the next two weeks the soldiers kept away; the nights were stirred only by familiar sounds: the roar of the waves, the hiss of nocturnal insects, the voices of people who came to the beach at odd hours of the night to smoke their joints of marijuana or to make love. Then one day in October I read about two unidentified female corpses that were found at Tarkwa Bay and Coconut beaches. Was Tay Tay one of them, I wondered? Had she met the violent, anonymous death I feared was her destiny?

That night, screams pierced the air again, a single woman's shriek, long and steady. There were male voices, too: barking at her, taunting, hooting, gloating, laughing lecherously. I did not stir but lay crouched against my boulder, unable to revive the rage and resolution that had provoked my pledge to Tay Tay. It was as if I had split into two persons: the man who had promised to stand up to the brutal rapists and the man who now listened to a woman's terrified screams with a sort of indifference.

Time passed and the bloody orgy ended. I heard the blast of the truck's exhaust, then the sputter of its engine as it drove away. A part of me desired to search in the dark for the woman left on the sand and try to help her. But another part of me dissented. Why endeavour to save the life of a woman already utterly destroyed? So that, till her dying day, she could endlessly relive and recount the horrors of that night? I did not move.

In the weeks that followed, the soldiers returned with regularity, sometimes with one screaming quarry, other times with more. I read news reports about female corpses found at other beaches, too. The accounts contained police theories of the killer's psychological portrait and likely motives. One theory was that he had contracted a serious venereal disease from a prostitute. Another, that he had been cheated out of money. Or he could be a religious fanatic waging a moral war against prostitution.

◆

I clearly remember the events of that morning when a young woman died on the beach and I was arrested, charged with rape and murder.

The night had been cold and dark as charcoal. I had spent it coiled up against the boulder, like a baby drawing warmth from a mother's body. Soon after the church bell rang four times, I heard the clatter of a truck pulling to a stop, then the shudder of a turned-off engine. A cold dread enveloped me. My heart thudded in my chest.

The voice of a woman being dragged, pleading, aroused a weak flame of anger inside me, but it quickly died away. Lethargic and weak-willed, I lay still. For two hours the fierce torrent of the woman's shrieks tore the night in two. After the soldiers' departure, my dread unthawed. Compelled by shame and guilt I decided to seek out the victim. Guided by her groans, I traced a path to her through the mist. As I approached her the bell at St Gregory's Cathedral chimed seven times. I bent over her and asked, 'Can you hear me?'

She stopped groaning. There was silence.

'Can you?' I said again.

She let out a shriek that stilled the wind. Then, in one wild motion, she bolted up and ran towards the waves, like one hastening to embrace a lover returned from afar. I wanted to shout after her that I was not one of her tormentors, but my tongue was glued to the floor of my mouth. As I watched, her faint figure disappeared in the mist. I heard a choked cry as she collided with the waves: a cross between a belated cry for help and a defiant dare to fate.

It was then that I ran after her, following the path she had cleared through the mist. I ran until a wave hit me. I reeled, then lowered myself into the cold water. I swam blindly, thrusting this way and that, drawn by her voice. Time seemed to stand still. I was already exhausted when I heard her cough just behind me. I lunged in the direction of the cough, then grabbed one of her legs. She kicked out with her free leg and hit my face. The stab of pain spread in widening circles inside my head. Dazed and out of breath, I was unable to swim properly for a while, but could only rise and fall with the rhythm of the waves. The woman's yelps grew fainter as the waves drew her further and further away. Eventually she became one with the mist, invisible. Too tired to go after her, I began to swim in the direction of the shore.

I was almost there when I saw a tall figure wading in. I recognised Lanky the lifeguard.

'Don't bother,' I muttered to him. 'Death's will is strong.'

He paid me no heed but ploughed on into the ocean. A short while later he began to shout instructions, to which the drowning woman responded with weak moans. Soon their voices ceased. Had the two of them met the same fate, overwhelmed by the ocean's power? I wondered. But in a moment Lanky appeared at the edge of the shore. The next wave deposited the woman's body at his feet. He pulled her out of the reach of the waves, then stood astride her and began to press on her belly. Faint snorty sounds came from her, followed by horrible gargles. I moved closer and observed the lifeguard at his work of resuscitation. I knew his efforts were in vain.

The sun broke through the mist and bathed the scene in pale light. The dying woman turned her head ever so slightly towards me. Her eyes were red, as if daubed in blood, but the expression on her face was turning into something radiant and peaceful. A smile.

I turned and walked away, ashamed of myself for yet another failure, another turning away from responsibility. What was my life but a succession of silences, evasions, abdications? I saw the panorama of my past projected as if on a large screen spread before my mind's eye. My mother. My father. My grandmother. Iyese. Tay Tay. Iyese again. And again.

Later, I saw from a distance that people had begun to gather around Lanky and the corpse. I could not resist the urge to return to the scene.

I listened to Lanky tell the dead woman's story. His gusto saddened me. For neither he nor his audience understood the dreadful and devious workings of power. They did not realise that for those who suffer in this life, the grave can possess a dark allure.

PART THREE

Malaise

Chapter Twenty-four

I had begun reading the story after I returned from work on a Friday evening. Engrossed in its twists and turns I did not stop to eat supper until, in the dead of the night, I read its last strange sentence – and by then a grumbly stomach had become the least of my worries.

I remembered the words of the sorceress I had visited last year in a desperate bid to unearth my biological roots. Like my other efforts, the visit had been a dismal failure – until this story illuminated my past in a way that made my heart tremble. Did the gods wish to punish me for casting a backward glance? For trying to crack open the kernel of forbidden mysteries? There was no immediate answer to these questions: Bande prison was closed to visitors at weekends.

Early in the morning I rolled out of bed and reached for the phone. My adoptive mother picked up after the first ring. Her 'hello' was the slur of somebody startled from sleep.

'It's Femi,' I announced without salutation.

'Is everything all right? Are you okay? You're not in any trouble, are you?' Four months ago, when she learned about my plan to move out to my own flat, she had cried and cajoled, afraid that something would go wrong: I would not eat well enough, or be able to keep the flat clean.

'Everything is fine. Well, most things,' I mumbled. 'I called to ask you a few questions.' Pausing to choose my words cautiously,

I heard the quickened rise and fall of her breath. 'Did you adopt me from the Langa Orphanage?'

Her reply bore the marks of irritation. 'Your father and I went out to a function at the Niger Club last night. Why do you wake me up from sleep to ask a question I have answered before?'

'I'm sorry,' I said formally. 'But I *really* want to be clear.'

'Yes, from there! Could I now return to sleep?'

'Does the name Iyese mean anything to you? Or Emilia?'

Silence.

'Was my mother named Iyese or Emilia?'

A short spell of silence. In the background, I heard my adoptive father's sleepy voice ask, 'Is he starting up with that crap again?' She hushed him. Then, in a hurt tone, she said, 'I see I'm no longer a mother to you.'

'I meant my biological mother.'

'I have told you that I don't have those details.' She sounded impatient.

'Was she a prostitute?'

Silence.

'Was she murdered?'

She gave a long sigh of exasperation. 'I really must go back to sleep.' Then I heard the click of the receiver as she hung up. For a few seconds I stared in disgust at the phone in my hand, buzzing with a dial tone.

I went to the wardrobe and rummaged in several trouser pockets until I found the marijuana cigarette I had been saving. Then I groped my way to the door and went outside. The morning was still grey and overcast. I struck a match and, with my left palm, shielded its flickering flame from the breeze while I lit the joint. I drew hungrily, letting the smoke slip down my throat and spread deeply inside me. Exhaling slowly, I was rocked by a sharp nausea. With a flick of the finger I tossed the burning roll onto the dewy grass. A wisp of smoke curled up from it and rose into the air.

I lay back in bed, my thoughts a series of disconnected waves. The only thing clear in my mind was the certainty that I could not bear to see Bukuru in person. A face-to-face would involve too much pain on my part; perhaps too much shame on his. Any further communication with him would be by letter, a less personal device. Without waiting for the outlines of the thought to be filled in, I fetched some sheets of paper. In a shaky hand, I began to scribble a letter I planned to send through Dr Mandi.

◆

Monday morning came, but rather than driving to Dr Mandi's office as I had planned, I found myself heading for Bande prison.

A very different journey from the first. The curiosity I had felt during the earlier visit had given way to a heaviness of spirit. I was grateful for the solitariness of the rough road, the absence of other traffic. My emotions, still very much in a flux, needed a wide empty space within which to sort themselves out.

How was I going to start once I entered Bukuru's cell? Give him the letter straight away? Let him read it, or read it to him? Perhaps just try to talk, saving the letter to give to him when I left? But would he talk? Under my accusing eyes, might he not clam up and back away? As for me, how much more of my past could I bear to disinter?

The prison superintendent was at a meeting. His secretary welcomed me with a warmth I found sadly ironic, then ran off to fetch a warder to escort me. She returned with a stocky man whose eyes shone evilly.

'Corporal Joshua will take you to the cell,' she said.

Joshua pitched groundnuts into his mouth, chewing with wide movements of the jaw, like a camel.

'You doctors no get fear,' he said outside the superintendent's office, the smell of roasted nut thick on his breath. 'You no fear to enter cell and talk with a madman. I strong, but I no fit talk to crazeman. That one pass me.'

◆

Confronted with Bukuru in the pathetic flesh, I was struck dumb by sensations I had no words to express. I avoided his eyes, afraid that engaging them would reveal to me a truth I half-wished not to learn.

At length he asked, 'Did Dr Mandi send you my story?'

'Yes,' I said.

'Did you find time to read it?'

'I read it over the weekend. That's why I've come to see you.'

His eyes glowed with the hunger of curiosity.

'It was dispiriting,' I said.

'It wasn't easy for me to write.'

'Your story ends where mine begins. That's why I have come today. To tell you my own story.'

'Your own story?' he echoed.

'I told you and Dr Mandi that I was one of life's underdogs. Remember?'

'Oh,' he said.

'Since twelve, I have been looking for a lost part of myself. For the door through which I came into the world. For the man and woman whose blood mingled to mould me. Simple things others took for granted. Until I read your story, I had no idea at all. I have come because I believe you may know the answers. But I should tell you my own story first.'

228

I handed him my letter. He furrowed his brows in bewilderment, then began to read.

◆

It was only ten years ago that I found out that I was an adopted child. It all began with a fight with my younger sister. When the fight was over, my life had changed. That's what drew me to the smiling corpse: it reminded me of the mystery of life. *My* life. I wanted to discover why somebody would die a hard death wearing a happy face.

For ten years I have experienced a recurrent dream in which a couple appear to me, sometimes sad, sometimes happy. Hardly ever in a hurry, they spend a long time with me, playing the games of my choice. When I ask, first the man, then the woman, 'Are you my father?' 'Are you my mother?' – then they vanish. The man disappears instantly, but the woman always hesitates. When I wake up the tears of my dream are still running down my face.

My life has been a stream cut off from its source, a story without a beginning. You know me as Femi Adero, but I was born with a different name. I was only a few months old when I was adopted into the Adero family. A physician by the name of John Adero became my father. His wife, Margaret Adero – a teacher – became my mother. They gave me the new name that I still bear today. Growing up, I never suspected there were things about my past buried in an unmarked grave and covered with the earth of my new history.

I never knew until I was twelve that I had been adopted.

◆

A little over a year ago I received a Christmas card from my then girlfriend, Sheri. My heart fluttered as I slit open the envelope. The card bore a printed message: MERRY CHRISTMAS TO A SPECIAL PERSON. Inside I found a folded blue sheet and spread it out. Then, over and over, I read the short letter, hoping – no, praying – that its words would somehow peel from the page and fly away. Instead they sank deep into my mind, hurting me with a pain fiercer than fire. They still echo inside my head:

> Separation is pain. I know how both of us had looked forward to spending our lives together as husband and wife after graduating from university. You also know that I am my parents' only child, that I am very close to them. I discussed our plans with my parents. Unfortunately, they are adamantly opposed to a suitor for me whose biological roots are uncertain. You must remember I told you how obsessive they are about their daughter pairing up with somebody with, quote and unquote, good genes. It tears my heart to leave you. I truly loved you. But I think it is best to draw back (but remain friends) since I do not see myself going against the wishes of my parents . . .

How could she so casually write words she must know would deeply wound me? And why wait three years into our relationship? The timing was particularly cruel. I was close to graduating, and looked forward to taking a job with the *Daily Chronicle*.

Cruel, too, though Sheri could not have known it, was her use of the phrase 'good genes'. Genes. That word has haunted me ever since the day I overheard my father use it in a conversation that had to do with me.

I was the favourite target of my four younger siblings –
two brothers and two sisters – whenever they hungered for
a fight, which was too often. They picked on me because,
as the oldest, I had to show restraint in my response. If I
lost my temper and manhandled any of them my mother
would reproach me for being a bully, for bloodying the
nose of a mere child. Sometimes I complained to my
parents of the advantage my brothers and sisters took of
my tied hands. In fairness to our mother, she always asked
them to leave me alone, though to no avail. Our father,
whom we all dreaded, chose to make light of my protests.
'You can't handle this small fart of a challenger?' he would
ask me, grinning. 'You were born with two strong fists. If
anybody is looking for your trouble, you should know
what to do.'

I knew what to do – only too well! But I also knew the
unwritten rule which unfairly required me not to do it.
Inevitably, the day came when I snapped.

A couple was visiting our parents from England – a
barrister who had been my father's best friend in
secondary school and who later studied law in England,
and his wife, an Indian-born English woman. They were
in Madia for four weeks and stayed in our house for the
first three days before setting out to see the rest of the
country. In anticipation of their visit our parents had
drilled us on the rules of good comportment. We were
not to stare at the visitors. We were not to raise our
voices during their stay. And, yes, fights were also
outlawed. My father warned that any breach would be
severely punished.

On the first day of the couple's visit, while they and our
parents sipped tea and reminisced, my youngest brother
sneaked up behind me where I sat reading a book and

dealt me a sharp blow to the back of the head. My first impulse was to make a small bundle of him and smash him against the wall. I overcame that temptation. I had little time to weigh the consequences of the next option before I got up and started on my way.

My parents and their visitors were laughing over some joke when I appeared in the doorway. Stopping sharply, I faced them, determined. For some time they continued to laugh, hardly seeming to take in my presence. Then they gradually wound down and focused their eyes on my face.

'I will kill Soochi if you don't stop him annoying me!'

'He will do what?' asked the lawyer as I made off through the door that led to the porch.

'Kill Soochi, I think he said,' his wife replied.

'But why?' asked the lawyer. 'Don't the other kids accommodate him well enough?'

'Of course, of course,' I heard my father say. 'But I warned Margaret early on that genes can be a most troublesome thing.'

'John, please!' my mother rebuked him. 'This is no time!'

I had made no sense then of the exasperation in my mother's voice. Genes had sounded in my ears as jeans, and I had been wearing a pair of jeans at the time. I sat outside the door sulking like an orphan, wondering what jeans had to do with it. Then my perplexity was replaced by a dread of the punishment that lay ahead for me – in two days, after the visitors had gone.

For the next two days I said little to anybody. I merely grunted in salutation whenever I encountered the adults. My parents accepted my terms; they grunted in return.

My father averted his eyes whenever our paths crossed, his lower lip clenched between his teeth, a man trying hard to contain his anger. The lawyer, too, was pretty taciturn, absorbed in his eternal tea-sipping. His wife, however, seemed to take my silent withdrawal as a personal challenge. One night, she drew me into an unexpected hug as I muttered a grudging good night. The following morning I made sure this time to keep my distance from her, wanting no repetition of her stifling hug.

One week after the visitors departed, the same heavy silence still pervaded the house. I was neither spanked nor scolded. My parents' faces wore a terrible scowl that seemed a cross between a grimace and a grin. In the tenseness of the silence I walked about the house with the guile of a cockroach, keeping to dark corners.

One morning my father called me as he got ready to go off to his clinic. With slightly shaky legs I entered the living room where he stood waiting.

'Good morning, Daddy.'

'Morning, Femi. I was wondering if my small man would help me carry my briefcase to the car?'

It was like the old, wonderful days once again! Carrying his briefcase to the car was an honour bestowed on me as the first child. Before getting into his car my father hugged me, then lightly kissed my forehead. He had done it countless times before, but that day it seemed to contain a special meaning. Tears of relief streaked down my face and my lips quivered with joy. I turned and walked back to the house. My mother stood in the centre of the entrance hall, a wide smile spread across her face.

'The praying mantis!' she said. Praying mantis – the playful name she called me whenever I was in a petulant

mood. Smiling through my tears, I ran to her for an
embrace. It was perhaps the happiest day of my life. I did
not suspect that my saddest day lay not far ahead.

◆

On 4 May 1978 I had a bloody fight with my immediate
younger sister, Eda. That fight keeled my life over and
took away everything that had kept me safe and stable.

Eda, who is a year and a half younger than I, had a
diabolical hunger for fights. She would goad me at every
opportunity until I obliged her with one. At last, the day
came when I ran out of patience with her. Give her one
real fight, I told myself, and she would learn her lesson.

The fight started with her favourite joke – to call me
'elephant ears'. After that she improvised a song about my
large ears and sang it in her high unmelodic voice. I let her
carry on for a while, but her long tuneless singing finally
frayed my nerves. I responded with my own stock insult:
'Your mouth is wide enough for a rickety *molue* bus to
drive in.'

She stopped singing and charged at me, landing me two
punches on the chin. The pain spread all over my face.
Enraged, I unleashed blows of my own. At first she was
shocked and puzzled. Then a demented smile lit her face
and she flung herself at me, missing most of her punches.
The ferocity of my blows soon overwhelmed her, and in
spiteful frustration she shouted, 'Bastard!' I heard the curse
only faintly, still hitting. Defenceless against my knuckles,
she cried again, 'Bastard! Bastard! Bastard! Bastard!'
Eventually her cries jolted me out of my possessed state.
Her battered face horrified me. Her upper lip was split
open, her right eye swollen shut. A slow stream of blood

flowed from her nose. A terrible fright shook my whole body. What would our parents do when they came home that evening and saw the wreckage I had made of my sister?

Eda touched her face and, in horror, inspected her blood-stained finger. As if she had seen the very picture of her own death, she squawked, then let out a fresh torrent of curses. 'Bastard! Son of the gutter! Wait till my parents come home. Today is today. You have to go back to the goatshed where you were born! Bastard picked up from the latrine! Evil child who entered his mother's womb through the back door! Today, you'll be returned to the gutter where you belong!'

That evening, our mother burst into tears as I recounted what had happened. She and our father had listened wearily as I described the trivial events that led to the fight, but when I told how my sister had called me a child of the gutter she began to cry. Confused, I looked at our father, but his face bore an expression of stony distance. I glanced at Eda. Her head was bowed. I knew she was avoiding our parents' eyes.

Then the meaning of this incident began to take a shape in my mind. Slowly at first, then at a shattering speed. The rush of knowledge became unbearable. I felt myself swooning. The room swirled out of focus. Then my legs disappeared from under me.

Why had I never noticed the differences between my siblings and me? It was not only the fact that I was light-skinned while they had a darkness of complexion obviously inherited from our mother. Or that they were rotund, while I was tall and skinny. Or that my eyes were deeper and more intense – and my ears larger. It was something else: our parents' odd counsel at family pep talks, their unfailing admonition to us, their children, to remember that we were equal in their eyes, none of us loved less than the others. That need to spell out something that should be obvious, why had I not been struck by the awkwardness of it? Why had I waited until this moment to be told by my mother's tears, my father's brooding muteness?

For the next few weeks I tried in many silent ways to get my parents to explain my past to me. My eyes held questions seeking answers. My parents saw them, but chose to respond with a stolid silence. Far from diminishing, my need to know increased, grew into an obsession. One day, alone with my mother, I decided to broach the taboo subject explicitly.

'Mother,' I said, for the first time feeling the word heavy in my mouth. 'Who are my *real* parents?'

She looked at me sharply. Then she gave me a nervous, uneasy smile. 'Don't you feel loved in this house? Are we now strangers to you?'

'Please!' I cried. 'I feel at home here. But I now know that you're not the mother who gave birth to me. I want to know the rest of the story.'

'You have been hurt,' she said. 'But love will heal your pain.' She came up and tried to cuddle me.

I pushed her away. 'If you love me, tell me what I ask.'

'Do you doubt that I love you?' she asked, stung by my words.

'No!'

'Because if you do, you mustn't. I love you.'

'A little thing is all I ask of you,' I pleaded.

'I don't have the information you want.'

'Tell me what you know. I'll go to Father for the rest.'

'He knows even less.'

Despite my disappointment I decided to approach my father. Early the next morning, while he was listening to the news, I joined him.

'Good morning, Dad.'

He turned, surprised. 'Morning, Femi. You're up early. How are you?'

'Bad.'

'Bad?' He fixed me with a perplexed look. 'What is the matter?'

'Who are my real parents?'

He swiftly turned off the radio. Then he regarded me with a cold, pained stare. At any other time those eyes set on me in that fashion would have taken away my courage, but not that day.

'I see,' he said finally, throwing his head upward. 'I see that we're no longer real enough for you. Your mother and I are now fake, eh?'

'I want to know who gave birth to me. Just to know.' I hated the shy sound of my voice.

'Listen, Femi. This is your home. We're your parents. We love you. Very much, if you need reminding. We'll support all your healthy pursuits. But searching for what is better left alone is not a healthy pursuit.'

The finality of his tone did not deter me. In the months that followed I pestered them with more questions, all of which met silence. Whenever they went out I pried through their papers. In vain. I went searching for the Langa Orphanage, but learned it was long closed. I wrote letters to several newspapers, but no responses came. The few clues I ever got were from my mother, tidbits that were of little value, tiny specks of light in the vast night of my ignorance.

As time passed I became resigned to not knowing. With

237

other interests to occupy me in the present, the desire to dig around in my past fell dormant. I was ill-prepared when it flared up again at the beginning of my second year at Madia University.

◆

I met Sheri in poetry class and fell in love, first with her poems, then with her eyes and the lilting voice that gave a seductive melody to her speech. She returned my interest with a charm and enthusiasm that flattered me. On our first date she led me to a wooded area behind her hall of residence. It was there, while we cuddled and kissed, that I told her about myself. Motivated by a desire to hide nothing, I related the story of how I found out that I was adopted and the pain of my fruitless search for my biological parents.

She assured me that none of this need be an obstacle to our relationship. Relieved, I let myself fall deeper and deeper in love.

I became worried when Sheri went home several times without discussing me with her parents. But she promised to talk to them as soon as we were sure about the direction of our relationship. In December 1986 I told her of my desire to marry her. She went to spend the holiday with her parents. From there she sent me a Christmas card and a letter with words that tore my heart out.

◆

Two days after receiving Sheri's letter I travelled to Jesha, a small dusty town forty miles outside Langa, to meet a famous sorceress. A friend of mine had sworn that this woman had the power to commune with the past and the future.

Her appearance was more bewildering than anything I had imagined, the most striking thing about her being her mammoth size. She sat on a wide wooden chair, her face lit with an expression of eternal patience. She could have been sitting there, on that one spot, since the beginning of time.

She watched with dark eyes as I stooped through the low wooden door and entered her shrine. The shrine was simple, clean and uncluttered, far from the jumble of roots, herbs, beads and animal hides my mind had pictured. The air was perfumed with incense and scented candles. The white garment worn by the sorceress gave her a chaste, holy look.

'Son,' she said without seeming to stir her body. 'You have come with a heavy load. Sit down.' With her eyes she indicated where. I sat down, wishing I had not come, hastily rehearsing how to make my excuses and flee.

'Son, your trouble is strong, but you have come to the wrong place. It is not for me to answer your questions.'

'Why not?' I asked.

'Because the answer you seek is small.'

'It isn't small to me,' I said. 'I wish to know who my natural parents are.'

'The ancestors who are wiser than all of us said a long time ago that a basket cannot cover a pregnancy. They spoke the truth for yesterday, today and tomorrow. If your trouble were as big as a pregnancy I would see the answer. But the answer you seek is like a pebble thrown into the belly of the big sea. I don't have the magic to recover such a pebble. None but the gods who inhabit the depths of the sea can do so. The gods have marked you out for great things, but they have also withheld the small things from your knowledge.'

'Why is that?' I asked in a vexed tone.

'Son, I am not privy to the decisions of gods.'

'But why can't you give me some light yourself? Why must my past be overcast?'

'Son, I have only this light to shed: don't let your spirit collapse over the small things. If you live long you'll be a great man and the small things won't matter any more. A great plan is laid out for you. None but yourself can derail it.'

I rose to leave, my face clouded with disappointment. She motioned me to sit back down.

'I speak to you now as one who could have been your grandmother if the gods had not decided that my womb would bear no children. Don't wrestle with fate, my son. To know is sometimes good, but to have the wisdom to accept what you cannot know is better.'

'You're saying that I'll never know about this? Never?'

'Who am I to say that? I am just a poor childless widow who fetches firewood for the gods. I am less than the fart from their rumps. Not even the gods speak the language of never. They only set the price for the choices we make.'

'If the answer to my past can be bought at any price, I am ready to pay it.'

'You speak with the voice of the young. You will grow to learn that knowledge is sometimes a weight to be borne. That's why a palmwine tapper never tells everything he sees from the high branches. He takes some of it to his grave. Go home, son.'

◆

That is my story. I am a man searching for his lost
pebble. I am a stream cut off from its source. Tell me,
if you know: where does such a stream go?

◆

Handing the sheets of paper back to me, Bukuru avoided my
eyes. A fit of anger stirred inside me.

'What kind of man would abandon his child?'

He coughed lightly, but did not speak. We stood in silence.
Then, feeling myself reeling, I spoke again.

'You're certain Iyese's son was removed to the Langa
Orphanage?'

'Yes,' he answered. His voice was husky, like a man fighting
a lump in his throat. 'That's what Violet told me.'

'I was adopted from that orphanage,' I said, as if he could
have overlooked this detail in my account!

He made a nasal sound, but kept a wary silence.

'Isn't Ogugua an Igbo name?' I queried.

He grunted his affirmation. 'Why do you ask?'

'My adoptive mother said I had an Igbo name when they
adopted me. That's one of the few things she told me. She didn't
say what the name was.'

'What are you suggesting?' His tone, to my shock, was less a
question than a rebuke.

'If my mother was a prostitute, that might be a reason my
adoptive parents would withhold information from me.'

'I don't know,' he said.

'If they knew my mother was murdered, then perhaps they
wouldn't want to tell me.'

'This is mere guesswork. There's no evidence at all. The
connections are not there.'

241

'You wrote about a gash in the baby's right leg. I carry the scar of such a wound.'

'A coincidence,' he said, still evading me.

Exasperated with this dodging and weaving, I began to soliloquise, addressing myself in a detached, disinterested voice. 'Your mother was a prostitute. You may never know your father because your mother slept with many men. She was raped and then she was murdered. You were found lying on top of her, a blood-spattered baby. You were taken to an orphanage from where you were adopted. You became Femi, a child forbidden to visit his past because it was full of terrors. You were warned, but you persisted. You wanted to find out what it was in your history that nobody would talk about. Now you know.' Pausing, I forced Bukuru to look me in the eye. 'Could you be my father?'

He leaned against the wall and shut his eyes. Silence. That familiar cop-out. Silence – again!

Chapter Twenty-five

Ten days later Dr Mandi phoned me at work. In a broken voice, he asked me to drive over to his office. 'Immediately, if you don't mind the short notice,' he said.

I arrived in about an hour. Corporal Joshua was there, sunk in a low chair, a file locked under his arm. Dr Mandi looked like a caricature of himself: ravaged, thin and sickly, his face dark and stretched.

'You must sit down,' he said. 'I'm afraid Joshua here has brought some terrible news. Tell him, corporal.'

'He done die,' the warder said.

'Who?'

'The suspect. MTS 1646.'

Dr Mandi caught my eye and gave a sorrowful nod.

With nervous speed my eyes travelled from the psychiatrist to the warder. 'How did it happen?' I asked.

Joshua didn't speak, so Dr Mandi said, 'Suicide. He hanged himself.'

'I don't believe it!' I shouted.

'I saw him only yesterday and there was no indication at all,' said the doctor. 'I actually thought his spirits were quite good. I told him I had finally met his old friend, Ashiki. We even discussed the possibility of my coming with Ashiki to see him next week. But now . . .' He threw his hands up in despair.

'I don't believe it,' I said again.

'Exactly my first reaction, too,' Dr Mandi answered. 'But it's true, I'm afraid. In fact, Joshua has brought a sort of suicide note. Addressed to you.'

Joshua heaved himself up and handed me the file. The handwriting was familiar. At the top of the first page was the caption, FINAL SILENCE.

Dear Femi,

I had wanted some time to reflect on our last painful meeting. But soon after your departure a powerful silence engulfed me. A monstrous and greedy silence, swollen with memories, it displayed before me my array of dead things: people betrayed, hopes dashed, dreams unfulfilled, roads forsaken, paths not taken.

Swish . . . wish . . . ish . . . sh! I felt a tremor in the still air, then dead quiet. A ghost's entrance into the membrane of silence. Whose ghost was it visiting me, I wondered, on this dark day? My father, perhaps. Then why did he not speak? He, a man who once dazzled me with the music of words? Speak, I whispered to the ghost, if you are my father. Say one of your strange words again. Braggadocio, again. Tintinnabulation. Hocus pocus. Brouhaha.

Are you my grandmother? I asked of the ghost. Or my mother? Or Iyese, returning to reproach me for a desertion of so long ago? Perhaps you are the drowned prostitute, pleading too late to be rescued – or come to summon me to another place.

Perhaps the visitor was a stranger's ghost, one of the multitude who had lived and died in this very cell. Died with their eyes wide open, their death unwitnessed, their last groan swallowed by the surrounding silence. Was it one such cellmate – one such soulmate – haunting the cell again to witness my own life slowly draining away?

Femi, I began to think about you. I felt a tightening in

my chest and interpreted it as grief. But grief was at once too complicated and too simple a word for the tearing I felt inside of me, the sense of being riven, sad and angry at the same time.

Could it be true that you are flesh of my flesh, blood of my blood? That we are linked, you and I, by a strange intersection of fate and probability? I have tried to imagine you as Iyese's son, to decide if you resembled either of us, or both. But I could not tell. Every familiar thing has become strange. Still, are not all humans, at bottom, mirages and mirrors? Mirages of faces in constant transfiguration, endlessly forming and reforming into multiple images. Mirrors of one another, reflecting now this stranger, now that, becoming one with every living person.

'Could you be my father?'

That was the question you asked me. I evaded it, but I should have given a simple answer: 'Yes. I am the man who abandoned you on a rainy day in a room where blood flowed from your wounded leg.'

Even if it was not you in that room. Even if I was not the baby's father. Whatever the complicated facts of biology might be, I should have been that boy's father that day. I should have tried to save him – you – as a father would. Or any decent human being. But I didn't. I was too afraid of involvement in others' intimate pain.

I live with the shame of that abdication in this cell. I am here because many years ago I fooled myself that the counterfeit coin of silence was good enough to buy peace of mind. I forgot my grandmother's wisdom, that the mouth owes stories the debt of speech.

I had hoped that telling my story would pacify the demons that inhabited my memories. Then your story

245

shattered my illusions: now I know that my story was unfinished. 'Could you be my father?' Henceforth, that question will haunt every breath I draw.

Do my genes flow in you? And if they do, would Sheri and her parents consider them good genes or bad genes? Good genes; bad genes. These are meaningless conceits, Femi, cloaks for human vanity. Only the mean-spirited make such anxious distinctions between the legitimate and the illegitimate, the chosen and the damned.

Dr Mandi came to visit me this morning. Joshua brought him to me (after a difficult beginning, Joshua and I have reached a strange sort of accommodation), but I was unprepared for the shock of what I saw when he shuffled in. Before me – after an interval of so few days – stood a drastically changed man, his eyes too large in his taut face, his body emaciated, his muscles wasted.

'My God!' I exclaimed. 'What happened to you?'

He told me that he is afflicted with a disease, as yet unidentified, that is eating him away.

'It must be scary,' I said with a shudder.

'Not at all,' he answered. 'Actually I am calm about it. I joked to my wife that at this rate she may find no body to bury when I die.' He laughed loudly. In my mind I pictured him dead, and in the picture he resembled my father.

'Let's not talk about death,' I said. 'I have been present at too many deaths.'

'All right, then. Let's talk about you.'

'What is there to talk about?'

'I finally met Ashiki. He appeared in my office yesterday. Quite a fellow.'

Stunned by the news, I asked, 'How does he look these days? What does he do?'

'You will find out for yourself. He wants to come and

see you, if it can be arranged. You know, he refused to shake my hand when he entered my office, but when he left, he slipped me a note. It said, "I will be in court on 15 March. Your testimony may or may not earn you my handshake." Which brings me to another subject.'

'Yes?'

'Your case. Illness has forced me to consider what is important and what is merely expedient. I have decided not to bear false witness in court.'

'But that means signing your own death certificate.'

'Either way, I'll die. I might as well die a death that will earn me some dignity. It is the least I owe to myself.'

He extended his hand for a parting handshake. I took it firmly, then relaxed my grip, alarmed by the frailness of his hand, the feel of his fleshless bones. No, I did not attempt to dissuade him. What was the use when he is caught in a system that requires of a man that he lie or die? Lie and die.

After his departure I calmly surveyed my future. What I saw was pitiful. In a few weeks a ride in a Black Maria back to Justice Kayode's courtroom. From the vehicle's barred window, a view of the crowd come to witness the resumption of something misnamed a trial. Inside the hot courtroom, sly prosecutors and suborned witnesses. Justice Kayode's judge's robe and gavel, his easy lies, his deceits and conceits that masquerade as law, order and justice.

The court would go through its motions, then deliver a guilty verdict. I would be sentenced to a term of imprisonment. Then, after months, perhaps only weeks, of incarceration in a sunless tomb – when it was safe to assume the world had forgotten about me – I would be disposed of once and for all, my dead body silently entombed.

247

Was that, I asked myself, a fate worth waiting for? Worth cutting Dr Mandi's life short for? Even if I were released today, how would I gain freedom from the ghosts that haunt me? From the memories of the many victims of my silence? From the guilt of turning away from a sleeping, bleeding child?

'Could you be my father?' you asked me, Femi. I don't know. I know I am a man who ran away from duty and love. A man who must point a finger at fear and say: this is what drove me to do what I did, the dreadful god in whose name I slayed my voice.

My grandmother was right: stories never forgive silence. My silence has no hope of redemption. It is too late in the day for me to look for grand insights. What I know are simple truths. I know that the fabric of memory is reinforced by stories, rent by silences. I know that power dreads memory. I know that memory outlasts power's viciousness. I know – as a man accused of rapes and murders I didn't commit – that a voiceless man is as good as dead.

It is better, I have decided, to go away quietly, and soon. I will ask Corporal Joshua a final favour, to carry to Dr Mandi a file containing this letter, these words addressed to you.